*To see how it all started, read*

# Three Girls
## in the City:

# Three Girls
## in the City
# BLACK AND
# WHITE

### By Jeanne
### Betancourt

SCHOLASTIC INC.
New York Toronto London Auckland Sydney
Mexico City New Delhi Hong Kong Buenos Aires

ISBN 0-439-49841-4

Copyright © 2003 by Jeanne Betancourt. Published by Scholastic Inc. All rights reserved.

SCHOLASTIC and associated logos are trademarks and/or registered trademarks of Scholastic Inc.

4 5 6 7 8 9/0

12 11 10 9 8 7 6 5 4 3 2 1

Cover and interior designed by Joyce White.

40

Printed in the U.S.A.
First printing, January 2004

## ACKNOWLEDGMENTS

Thank you to Nicole Betancourt, Olivia Branch, Rebecca Johnson, Jazan Higgins, Teri Granger Martin, Manuela Soares, Sherry Morris, and Kibra Yohannes for their insightful readings of this manuscript.

# TABLE OF CONTENTS

Broadway

34th St.

11th Ave.
10th Ave.
9th Ave.
8th Ave.
7th Ave.
6th Ave.
5th Ave.

23rd St.

Chelsea

17th St.

14th St.

EAST RIVER

3rd Ave.
2nd Ave.
1st Ave.

GReenwich Village

8th St.
4th St.

East Village

NEW JERSEY

E. Houston St.

W. Houston St.

Soho

Little Italy

HUDSON RIVER

TRibeca

West Broadway
Church St.
Broadway
Lafayette

Canal St.

Chinatown

Chambers St.
**J·D**

◻◻

N
W · E
S

BROOKLYN

Battery Park

Statue of Liberty

**MANHATTAN**
**IN NYC**

Scale: 1 mile

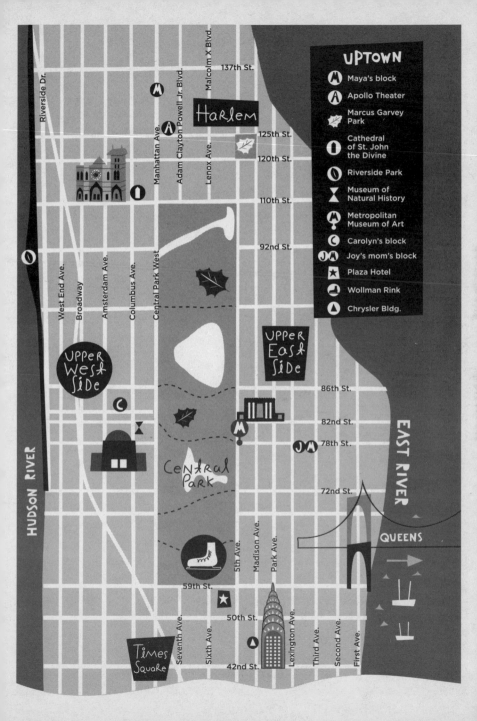

# Three Girls
## in the City

BLACK AND WHITE

# Remember Me

Maya Johnson ran across 125th Street.

A police car was stopped at the corner. "Hey, Maya, where's the fire?" one of the police officers called to her. "Slow down. Okay?"

Maya recognized him. He was a cop friend of her cop dad. She slowed down and smiled back at him.

Her mother's vintage clothing store — Remember Me — was in the middle of the block. A banner reading BLOW-OUT ANNUAL CLEARANCE SALE — SATURDAY was stretched across the front window. Five customers were already lined up, waiting to get in. Maya glanced at her watch. It was 9:30 A.M.

She heard a tall woman with a short Afro tell the woman behind her, "I have my eye on a gold Dior gown from the seventies. I am *not* going to miss it."

"All I'm wanting is this fuzzy pink sweater set with a little pearl thing happening down the front," said the other.

"That would be from the fifties," said the first woman.

Maya went into the store and looked around.

The space was crammed with racks of clothes, shelves of hats, rows of shoes, and cabinets of jewelry. Boxes waiting to be unpacked stood in a corner. The day of the annual clearance sale was the busiest day of the year at Remember Me.

I'll help until eleven-fifteen, Maya decided, then I have to go downtown for my photography workshop. If I'm back up here by four, I can help with sales until closing time.

She breathed in a woodsy lavender smell and thought, Gran must be here with her incense sticks.

At that moment Josie appeared from behind a tall rack. She held out a burnt-orange stretch top. "I just pulled this for you and there you are."

Jay-Cee walked toward them, her arms piled high with satin jackets. "That top will look really good with your skin color, M," she said. "I found a pair of bell-bottoms for Carolyn in pastel stripes. And a black gauze-and-lace skirt for Joy. Carolyn and Joy are coming back with you after your photography thing, right? Gotta hang these jackets up." She'd said it all in one breath and left for the back of the store without waiting for answers.

Maya and Josie exchanged a smile. Jay-Cee was one of the most energetic and positive people they knew.

Josie took Maya's hand and gave it a little tug. "Your mother asked me to rearrange the hats. Help me."

"Maya Johnson!" Maya's mother's voice boomed through the store. Maya looked around until she spotted her mother's head above a rack of gowns. "Could you help me move these racks?"

Maya looked back to Josie. "Go," her grandmother said. "I can manage."

Carolyn Kuhlberg and her dad sat at the kitchen counter eating their Saturday breakfast. Orange juice, scrambled eggs, and fresh bagels — pumpernickel for him and raisin for her. He was reading the front section of the *New York Times*. She flipped through the rest of the paper looking for movie ads and reviews.

"After the workshop, I'm going to help at Mrs. Johnson's store," Carolyn reminded her father.

He looked at her over the rim of his reading glasses. "If Maya invites you to stay overnight, it's okay with me. As long as her mother or father is there." He went back to the paper.

Carolyn thought, He *wants* me to have a sleepover. Is it another clue that he has a girlfriend?

She bit into her bagel and reviewed the Dad-has-a-girlfriend evidence so far. One: A message on Dad's cell phone from a woman who told someone she called "darling" to meet her at seven o'clock that evening. Two: At seven that same night Dad left the apartment. He said he was going to his office in the Museum of Natural History. I watched from the apartment window. He went in the direction *away* from the museum. Three: I found a note he wrote reminding himself to BUY FLOWERS FOR M. G. Three clues that led to one conclusion. Dad is secretly seeing a woman with the initials M. G. Does he want me to stay at Maya's so he can stay out late with M. G.? I hope he doesn't tell me about M. G. If he does, I'll have to meet her and deal with it. What if he holds hands with M. G. in front of me? Or kisses her? I don't want him to tell me he has a girlfriend.

She took a swallow of juice and checked how he'd dressed for his day off. Jeans. A gray-green shirt that matched his eyes. She caught a whiff of men's cologne. He never wears cologne, she thought. More evidence?

"So you'll let me know if you're staying at Maya's," he said, interrupting Carolyn.

"Okay." She watched him sip his coffee and thought, Mom's dead. I know he loved her. So how can he go out with someone else?

He looked over at her, stared really. "You look upset. Is something bothering you, Carolyn?"

"No."

Joy Benoit-Cohen stood on a chair to reach her closet shelf. Wasn't her old camera in here some-place? She wouldn't be using her new digital camera for the photo workshop on darkroom technique. The instructor, Beth, wanted her to use a regular camera that made old-fashioned negatives. Joy had been tempted to skip the unit on darkroom. She told herself that printing with chemicals in a darkroom was old-fashioned. Digital and Photoshop were the way to go.

But if I don't take photography with Maya and Carolyn, I'm afraid we might not all stay friends. So I need my old camera. Where is it?

She searched behind shoe boxes and storage bags of summer clothes. It wasn't there.

Maybe it's in my bedroom at Dad's, she thought as she climbed down from the chair. She caught her reflection in the closet door mirror. Short dark brown hair. Almost black. Big brown eyes. "Your big eyes are your best feature," her mother liked to tell her. I have a big body, too, thought Joy. She turned to the right and left, studying her shape.

Guys on the street commented on her body sometimes.

Guys she didn't even know.

Guys she wouldn't want to know.

Well, I'm not going to hide under baggy clothes just because some guys are idiots, she reminded herself.

Her mother came into the room. "Don't you have to leave for your workshop soon?"

Embarrassed at being caught looking in the mirror, Joy banged the closet door shut. "I was just looking for my old camera. I think it's at Dad's."

Her mother sat on the edge of the bed. "Speaking of your father, I'm afraid you're going to have to stay there for a week next month. Sorry."

Joy had split her time between her divorced parents' homes since she was six. But she had gotten sick of living in two places. Besides, she hadn't liked her father's new wife or being the built-in babysitter for their toddler son, Jake. So now she was living only with her mother. She squatted and opened the bottom drawer of her bureau. Maybe the camera was in there.

"Where you going, Mom?" she asked.

"To the Caribbean. St. Barts. We're shooting a bathing-suit ad campaign there."

Joy felt something hard in the back of the drawer. Her old camera! She pulled it out and looked up at her mother. "We went to St. Barts when I was little," she remembered. "To that resort."

"That's right," agreed her mother. "This will be the first time I'm back there since I went with you and your father."

"Here's a weird coincidence," Joy said as she dropped the camera into her backpack. "Dad's taking me to St. Barts when I'm on spring break."

"With that wife and child?" asked her mother.

Joy nodded.

"I'm sure St. Barts will be filled with happy memories for your father." The words oozed with sarcasm. She sighed. "I wouldn't go back there if I didn't have to. We fought during that entire vacation. You were only five, so you probably don't remember."

But Joy did remember. Meals when her parents didn't speak to each other. Afternoons by the pool with Mom while Dad went for walks. On the beach with Dad while Mom stayed by the pool. Watching other kids having fun with both their moms and dads while hers avoided each other.

"So you'll stay with your father for that week," her mother was saying. "It'll go by quickly."

"Fine." Joy zipped her backpack closed and thought, I'm sort of looking forward to going to Dad's. Jake's walking now and is really cute. She glanced at the clock radio on her bedside table. Eleven-forty. The workshop started at noon.

"I'm going to Maya's mother's secondhand store after the workshop," she reminded her mother. "We're going to help with a big sale. And buy stuff."

Her mother retied the ribbon on Joy's old teddy bear. "A girl whose dad can afford vacations in St. Barts doesn't have to buy secondhand clothes."

Joy ignored the comment. "Gotta go," she said as she put on her jean jacket.

Her mother stood. "Don't forget I've got a business dinner tonight. I'll be home by ten. Call my cell when you get home. You can order in."

Joy left. Going down in the elevator she thought, Dinner alone tonight. Again. Maybe Maya would invite her to stay for dinner. She hoped so. Otherwise the night would be boring, boring, boring.

"Do you want a cab, Miss Benoit?" the doorman asked.

"Yes, please," she answered.

Sometimes it was handy having rich parents.

When Maya got off the train at Eighth Street, she spotted Carolyn on the subway platform. She called her name and ran to catch up. They climbed the stairs to the street together.

"We were on the same train," Carolyn commented happily.

"If we always get on the third car from the front," Maya suggested, "we'll know if we're on the same train *while* we're on it."

Carolyn grinned in agreement.

As they crossed Astor Place, Maya spotted Joy getting out of a cab. She called her name, but Joy didn't hear. She nudged Carolyn. "Do it, CK."

Carolyn put two fingers in her mouth and blew three sharp blasts.

Joy turned, spotted them, and waved.

When the three friends walked into the workshop together, Beth Bernstein was saying, "Take a seat. We have a lot to do today. I want to get started." The three girls joined four other kids at the long table.

Joy noticed that Beth had posted black-and-white photos on the wall behind her.

Maya looked around to check out who else was there. Two familiar faces — Charlie and Janice — and two new ones. Beth introduced them — Jennifer and Ron. Everyone said "Hi" and introduced themselves.

"So, guys," Beth continued, "in this workshop we're taking pictures in black and white and printing them in the darkroom. You all knew that coming in." She looked from Joy to Janice. "You two have been working in digital. You can either stay with us and use a regular camera or skip the next eight weeks. So you're with me, Janice?" asked Beth.

"I can't wait to learn darkroom," answered Janice.

"I appreciate your enthusiasm, Janice." She turned to Joy. "And you, Joy?"

"I can't wait either," Joy said in a bland voice.

Everyone, except the new kids, laughed.

Beth discussed the black-and-white photographs she had on display.

During the second half of the session, she brought them all into the darkroom. First she demonstrated how to make a print. She used the negative of a photo she'd taken of the outside of the media center. Then she gave them each a negative of the same shot and took them step-by-step through the process of making a print themselves.

When they were at the conference table she announced, "Next week we'll meet at a gallery in Brooklyn where a friend of mine has a show. He'll be there to discuss his work with you." She gave directions to the gallery and they all wrote them down.

Carolyn looked at Charlie's open notebook. He was printing the directions in big block letters. So he can see them, she thought. She remembered, in the first workshop, Charlie had told them that he had an incurable eye disease. His eyesight was already pretty bad and he would probably go blind. He said he was taking photography so he would look carefully at things while he could still see them. What is it like for him in the darkroom? she wondered.

Beth gave each of them a dozen rolls of black-and-white film. "In two weeks, bring in at least one roll of processed negatives and a contact sheet," she said. "See you all in Brooklyn next week."

Charlie turned to Carolyn. "Do you know what you're going to shoot?"

Carolyn put the rolls of film in her bag. "I don't have any ideas. Do you?"

"I have an idea," Charlie said. "Sort of. I hope it works."

"What's your idea?"

"If it works, I'll show you," he answered.

"Ready?" Joy asked Carolyn.

Carolyn hitched her bag over her shoulder. "See you next week, Charlie."

"In Brooklyn," he reminded her.

"Right." She was already several feet away when she turned and smiled back at him. Can he see me smile? she wondered.

The three girls stood in the crowded subway car that rushed northward through Manhattan. "Jay-Cee put aside some clothes she thought you guys would like," Maya told them.

Carolyn thought about Jay-Cee's personal style — tight, short, and bold. She liked that style — on Jay-Cee. "What did she pick out for me?" she asked.

"Great stuff!" Maya answered enthusiastically. "A black lace bustier thing and hip-hugging short shorts. In red leather."

"Oh," said Carolyn with quiet alarm.

"You could wear black fishnets with that," Joy said with a grin.

"And spike-heeled boots," added Maya.

Carolyn finally got it and grinned back. "R-i-i-ght," she drawled. "That outfit will be perfect for the big party at my dad's museum next week. He was just saying I should get something new for it."

Joy laughed. "You're catching on, CK."

Maya's mother put the three girls to work the moment they walked into the store. There were still two hours left of the big sale, and the store was a wreck. Carolyn helped Jay-Cee organize the sweater and T-shirt shelves. Maya and Joy folded and hung up already-tried-on clothes. Josie put them back on shelves and racks.

"It looks like it's been busy," Maya observed.

"It's been beyond busy," answered Josie. "More people than ever are buying secondhand. It always happens in hard times."

Maya held up a bright pink wool suit with a short jacket. It looked like something Jacqueline Kennedy would have worn in the sixties. "This isn't just any old secondhand clothing. Mom's stuff is vintage. It's practically antique."

"Like me," laughed Josie. "That was my suit, Miss M."

"Oops," Maya said. She put the suit back on the rack. "It's nice."

Joy came out of the dressing room in a black gauzy skirt and a black top with a scoop neckline and long, flared sleeves.

"That looks great on you!" exclaimed Maya.

Jay-Cee tied a black vinyl choker around Joy's neck. "Vamp/Goth works with her pale skin."

"What do you think?" Joy asked Carolyn.

Before Carolyn could answer, a boy's voice piped up. "You look like vampire. Very good look." Carolyn turned and faced Serge. Serge's friend, Alex, was right behind him.

Serge grinned, his face jewelry sparkling in the store's bright light.

Joy noticed that his bleached hair and purple streak were growing out. His true hair color was brown.

The girls had met Serge soon after they'd met one another. They all liked him. Maya had photographed him for a workshop assignment. During the second workshop, she photographed his friend Alex having his tongue pierced. "I didn't know you guys were coming to this sale," she said.

Alex held up a postcard advertising the Remember Me sale. "You sent us a card."

"My mother sent that card because you shopped here before," Maya explained. "It went out to all of her customers."

"Oh," said Alex, a little deflated. "We're just hanging out, anyway. Seeing some guys up here."

Jay-Cee straightened the shoulder on Joy's blouse. "Joy-ful, you *have to* get this outfit. Wear real pointy shoes with it and put black around your eyes. I'll show you how."

"And spike your hair a little," added Maya.

Joy glanced at herself in the mirror again. She liked how she looked — dramatic. "Would black jeans go with this top?"

Jay-Cee thought for a second. "They'd work, but bell-bottoms would be better. Just be sure everything is black."

"I think bell-bottoms would work better, too," Alex observed, imitating girl-speak. "What do you think, Serge?"

Serge took him seriously. "Yes, I think that is good. Very excellent style."

Alex stepped back and gave Serge a you-must-be-kidding look.

"He's just learning English," Joy said to Alex. "Cut him some slack."

"Cut me slacks?" Serge asked, confused. "*Slacks* means *pants*." He turned to Maya. "Does your mother sew clothes, too?"

"No," answered Maya, trying not to laugh. "Slack is a slang word."

"It means to give someone room. Like when they make mistakes," added Joy.

"We have some really great suits for men," Maya told Serge. "I'll show you." She looked over her shoulder. "You too, Alex."

"I don't wear suits!" protested Alex.

"Try one just for fun," said Jay-Cee. "I want to see."

While the boys went to the men's suit section with Maya, Joy went to the changing room. Carolyn brought tried-on things to Josie so she could re-hang them, and Jay-Cee went back to folding T-shirts.

Carolyn heard Shana's voice before she saw her. "I didn't think you'd be here. Don't you have photography class on Saturdays?" Carolyn looked up and saw that Shana was talking to Maya, not to her. Delores, another of Maya's other old neighborhood friends, was with Shana.

Maya heard the annoyance in Shana's voice and frowned. "The workshop ends at three o'clock."

Carolyn thought, Shana's even rude to Maya, who is supposedly her best friend. And she always seems angry. Grandpa would say she has a chip on her shoulder. Well, I'm not going to let her ruin my day.

Maya was thinking about Shana's rudeness, too. It hurt to have her oldest and best friend angry at her. Shana, her eyes narrowed, was silently looking from her to Serge. Does she think Serge is my boyfriend? wondered Maya. My *white* boyfriend? That would just make her angrier. Let her be angry. She was feeling angry herself. At Shana.

"Hey, Shana," Jay-Cee called. "You wanting some cool T-shirts? There's one that says, 'The revolution is now!' It's from forever ago."

While Shana was looking at the shirts with Jay-Cee, Alex came out of the dressing room in a fifties pin-striped suit. A fedora was perched on his cornrowed head. He thrust his arms in hip-hop moves and grinned.

"That is way cool, dude!" exclaimed Serge in his Russian accent. Joy and Carolyn exchanged a grin. Serge was trying so hard to be an American teenager.

"I thought it would look good on you," said Maya. Shana and Jay-Cee came back with the T-shirt.

Jay-Cee nodded approvingly at Alex. "You should get it."

"To wear where?" he asked.

"Alex?" Shana exclaimed. "Is that *you*?"

"Shana," said Alex, recognizing her. "Yeah, it's me." He grinned. "Is that *you*?"

"Mostly," she teased. "You been gone a long time."

"But not so far away," Alex said. "I only moved to Brooklyn."

Shana smiled. "I was in third grade and you were in fourth when you left."

"Ri-ight," agreed Alex. He sauntered toward her, his hands in the suit pants pockets. "How's things at three fifty-four?"

"Same old stuff. Heat was off most of the winter. Super's so busy dealing he doesn't notice. You and your brother still breakin' in the subways? You guys were fine."

Alex laughed. "Nah."

Carolyn remembered Alex break-dancing when he and his then-girlfriend, Wren, crashed a party at Joy's. "Alex dances great," she blurted out.

Shana shot her a mean close-your-mouth look. Carolyn did. But she didn't look away from Shana.

Shana looked away first. Back to Alex.

He didn't buy the suit, but he did get the fedora. Serge bought a satin jacket that said Hudson Falls Roller Rink on the back. Before the boys left, Maya noticed that Shana exchanged phone numbers with Alex.

Shana got the T-shirt that read THE REVOLUTION IS NOW! and Delores bought three T-shirts that didn't say anything.

It was after 6:00 P.M. and the store was officially closed.

"You coming with us, girl?" Delores asked Jay-Cee.

"Where you all going?" Jay-Cee asked back.

"Around," Delores answered. "There's an open mike at the center tonight."

"I'm down there!" said Jay-Cee.

Maya was about to say, "Me, too," when she remembered Joy and Carolyn. She couldn't bring them. It'd be kids from around the way. Not a scene for a cowgirl from Wyoming and a rich girl from the Upper East Side. Besides, Shana was on her case about having white friends, and she would make sure it was no fun if Maya brought them. But she hated not going.

After Maya's friends left, Joy decided to get the skirt and top she'd tried on, plus a pair of black velvet bell-bottoms and a black crocheted vest. Carolyn took the striped pants Jay-Cee picked out for her and a green sweater set that everyone said matched her eyes. Mrs. Johnson gave them 50 percent off the sale price as a thank-you for helping out.

Carolyn's cell phone rang. She didn't recognize the number that flashed on the screen.

"Hello," she said into the phone.

"Hello."

It was her father. Is he calling me from M. G.'s cell phone? she wondered.

"When are you coming home?" he asked. "Did Maya invite you to sleep over?"

"No."

"I see. When will you be home then?" She pictured him checking his watch to see what time it was. He was always checking his watch.

"When I said," answered Carolyn. "Remember, I said seven."

"All right then," he said. "See you at home." She heard disappointment in his voice. "Make sure Maya walks you to the subway."

As soon as Carolyn hung up, Mrs. Johnson invited her and Joy to stay for pizza.

"As a thank-you for helping," added Maya.

Carolyn looked at her watch. It was 6:30. "I should go now."

"I can stay," said Joy with more enthusiasm than she wanted to show.

Maya hesitated. If Carolyn and Joy both left, maybe she could catch up with her old friends. Why did she always have to choose between her old and new friends? She noticed a flash of hurt in Joy's eyes and realized that to Joy the hesitation meant she didn't want her to stay without Carolyn.

"That's great you can stay, Joy," Maya quickly said. "I'm for pepperoni on the pizza. What about you?"

Joy shrugged. "Pepperoni's okay. Whatever. I don't care."

"Can you guys walk me to the subway first?" Carolyn asked. "My dad —"

Maya threw an arm around her shoulder. "Course we can."

"We'll be your bodyguards," teased Joy. "I wish you could stay."

Carolyn picked up her Remember Me bag. "Me, too."

Maya followed them out of the store. Carolyn and Joy were both great in their own ways. She really liked them. If Carolyn and Joy were black, would Shana still be angry that they are my friends? Maya wondered.

# Museum of Natural History

Carolyn followed Maya and Joy out of the subway.

"This is the first time I've been to Brooklyn," she said excitedly.

Joy turned to her. "No it's not."

"You went to Brooklyn when you took the wrong subway and ended up in Coney Island," Maya reminded her. "Which is in Brooklyn."

"Are we near Coney Island? I'd love to go on that roller coaster again."

Joy shook her head. "Coney Island is in a whole different part of Brooklyn. There are a lot of different neighborhoods."

"And this one is called DUMBO." Carolyn remembered. "But I forgot what it stands for."

"For Down Under the Manhattan Bridge Overpass," Maya reminded her.

Carolyn looked up at the immense span of bridge above them. It reached across the East River to Manhattan. "The Manhattan Bridge is *huge!*" she exclaimed.

"Actually, that's the Brooklyn Bridge," Joy said, correcting her. "The Manhattan Bridge is behind you."

While Carolyn and Maya looked at the two bridges, Joy stared across the river at the space in the sky where the Twin Towers used to be. I'll never get used to them not being there, she thought. Even when some new big building takes their place.

Carolyn tugged Joy's sleeve. "People are walking across the Brooklyn Bridge! That must be an incredible view."

"It is," agreed Maya. "My history class walked across last year. It was great. Let's walk over it on the way home."

Carolyn shouted, "Yahoo!"

Joy couldn't resist imitating her. "Yahoo!"

Joy — in her Goth/Vamp look — yahooing like a cowboy, cracked Carolyn up.

On their way to the gallery, the three friends walked cobblestoned streets past restaurants, coffee shops, clothing stores, and old warehouses that had been converted into apartments and art studios.

It's a lot like the East Village, thought Joy. Maybe when I'm on my own I'll live in DUMBO. I bet my parents would buy me a condo. It'd be so much fun if Carolyn and Maya lived here, too. Maybe we could be roommates. Will we still be friends then?

Sometimes it felt to Joy like they were all three great friends and sometimes it felt like Maya and Carolyn were becoming best friends and she was just tagging along. I'm going to that big-deal event at the Museum of Natural History tonight with Carolyn and her dad, she reminded herself. Did Carolyn invite Maya first and Maya couldn't go? Was I second choice?

"I like how one bridge is named for Manhattan and one for Brooklyn," observed Carolyn. "Since they connect the two places. It's sweet and fair."

"You're sweet and fair," said Maya.

"Fair-ly corny," teased Joy.

"Here's the gallery," announced Maya, stopping in front of an old warehouse.

Joy thought the photographs were interesting. They were all of people who collected things. One person — an elderly gentleman — collected cans of soup. The photographer said some of the cans were fifty years old. The photograph showed the collector standing proudly in front of row upon row of soup cans. Another subject — a woman — collected shoes. Carolyn noticed that all the shoes were high heels. One guy collected matchbox cars.

After they'd all had a chance to look at the photos, they sat on the floor in the middle of the gallery. The photographer walked around and talked about his pictures. Joy thought he was a much better photographer than he was a speaker.

Maya asked the photographer how many times he had printed each photo before he produced a print that satisfied him.

He answered, "It depends. For most of these pictures, I printed a lot."

Charlie asked him why he wanted to photograph collectors.

"Seemed like a good idea at the time," he answered. "I thought they might sell. But they haven't." He looked discouraged. "Not much is selling these days. Bad times, economically." He turned to Beth. "Do they know what I'm talking about?"

"Of course they do," Beth answered. "They do live in the real world, Carl." Joy could tell she was disappointed in her photographer friend.

They went to a few other galleries with Beth. One show was of color photos taken in Cuba. Wonderful color, thought Maya. She knew that there hadn't been many changes in Cuba in almost fifty years. She loved looking at the architecture and old cars.

The other show was black-and-white underwater photography. "I would love to take pictures like these," Janice told Carolyn. "Just of nature. Pictures without people."

Me, too, thought Carolyn. Only I'd take them aboveground. From the mountaintops back home. I'd take pictures of birds in the sky instead of fish in the sea.

Walking across the Brooklyn Bridge, Carolyn thought of the mountains again. Views in every direction. The wind swirling around you. It made her feel like she could run, arms outspread, and fly. Be a bird herself.

Maya stopped at the railing and looked out. She spread her arms. "Being up here makes me want to fly."

A little thrill tingled up Carolyn's spine. She and Maya had had the same thought at the same time. She tried to remember if she and Mandy had shared thoughts like that. Maybe they had. But at the moment she couldn't remember any.

"If I could fly," Joy said, "I'd go directly to this Chinese restaurant I know on Mott Street."

"I'm hungry, too," agreed Maya. "Let's move it."

As they picked up the pace, Joy softly recited a chant that her Uncle Brett taught her. They'd chant it when she got tired during her walks with him. "Left. Right. Left, right, left. Had a good job and I left . . . , left." Maya and Carolyn joined in. "Did I do right? Left. Right. Left." Joy was surprised that they both knew it. "Left. Left. Left, right, left. Had a good job . . ."

The singsong of the chant reminded Maya of the poetry slam her grandmother told her about. It was next Saturday, with neighborhood teens performing their original poetry for points. Some of the poetry, Maya knew, would be like the lyrics to hip-hop — which she loved.

"You should bring Joy and Carolyn to the slam," Josie had said in her I-know-what's-best-for-you voice. "Carolyn will definitely get a kick out of it. I bet it'll remind her of cowboy poetry." Maya didn't ask Josie what cowboy poetry was. She was too confused about whether or not to invite Carolyn and Joy. They'd been to the house and her mother's store. But Maya had never brought them to a neighborhood thing before. And the slam was in the hall of the Abyssinian Baptist Church — right in the heart of Harlem. Josie, who had given Maya's hair a little pull, said, "You'll figure it out," and gone back to her own apartment.

But I haven't figured it out, Maya thought as she walked off the bridge with Carolyn and Joy. If I bring them to the slam and Shana comes, there will be more trouble between us. A ripple of anger went through Maya. No one can tell me I can't be friends with someone because of color. Not Shana. Not anyone. Period. Amen. The end.

But it wasn't the end, and Maya knew it. Not when her oldest and best friend disapproved of her new friends. New friends who were — day by day — becoming better friends.

"The restaurant is quite a few blocks from here," Joy said. "Let's take a cab."

"I don't mind walking," said Carolyn.

"Me, either," added Maya. She was already worried that she didn't have enough money on her for their Chinese snack.

But Joy had already hailed a cab. "Since I'm the only one who wants to ride, I'll pay for it." The cab pulled up in front of them.

Maya and Carolyn exchanged a glance that said, It must be fun to be rich, and climbed in.

Maya was sharing steamed dumplings and cold

sesame noodles with Carolyn and Joy when she brought up the subject of the slam. "There are judges selected from the audience," she explained. "They give each poet points from one to ten. Sometimes the whole audience judges which poet is best by how much they applaud. Usually the MC is a poet, too. The MC's job is to keep the whole thing moving along. Oh, yeah, and sometimes the poets work in teams."

"We had a slam in sixth grade," Joy remembered. "It was fun." She turned to Carolyn. "Judging poetry must sound weird to you."

Carolyn swallowed a mouthful of noodles. "It's just like a cowboy poetry competition."

"Cowboy poetry?" asked Joy, surprised. "What's that?"

"Well, darling," said Carolyn imitating a sophisticated New Yorker, "cowboy poetry is the type of poetry preferred by the westerner." She took a long puff of a straw-as-cigarette. "While it's not Shakespeare, cowboy poetry is quite wonderful in its own way, with references to cattle and the ranch and the life of the — well, yes, you guessed it — the cowboy. Quite quaint, really."

Maya grinned at her. "Do you know any cowboy poetry by heart?"

"We have to hear some," added Joy.

Carolyn tapped the straw on the table and thought. Finally, she said, "Here's one my grandfather made up:

*"Shadows fall across the rodeo ring*
*Where once I rode and roped and did my*
    *cowboy thing.*
*I was a real big deal, top in my class,*
*Until I leaned too far in the saddle and fell*
    *on my ass.*
*I learned my lesson, of course.*
*It's not the cowboy who wins the ribbons—*
*It's the horse.'"*

Joy laughed so hard ginger ale came out her nose. Maya and Carolyn saw it and cracked up.

"Your grandfather wrote that?!" Joy asked.

"He didn't win any prizes with it," admitted Carolyn. "But he always got a laugh."

Maya wiped away a tear with the back of her hand. "It's really good."

A memory flashed through Carolyn's mind like a home movie. Her mother in the hospital bed. Her grandfather sitting close by, reciting cowboy poetry. Her mother was unconscious by then. But her grandfather said that she might still be hearing him. "I'm only reciting the ones she really loved," he'd whispered to Carolyn. She shook away the sad memory with thoughts of the future. It would be fun to go to a slam. She'd tell her grandfather all about it.

Maya looked from Joy to Carolyn and wondered if she was making a mistake inviting them to the slam. Maybe it would have been better for everyone if she kept her neighborhood friends separate from her photography friends.

"Do you think your dad will let you go?" Maya asked Carolyn, half hoping she'd say no. Hoping, too, that Joy would have to babysit for her half brother that night or have dinner with her dad.

"I think he'll let me," answered Carolyn. "As long as I don't get home too late."

"Tell him it's cowboy poetry," suggested Joy, "*urban* cowboy poetry,"

"I have an idea of what I'm going to shoot in black and white," Maya said to change the subject. She hoped they'd forget about the slam and that she'd invited them.

Joy twirled the last of her noodles with chopsticks. "What?"

"I'm going to take pictures around my neighborhood. There are lots of changes going on. It won't look the same for long. It'll be neat to shoot in black and white because that's how the old pictures of Harlem look."

"That makes sense," agreed Joy.

"It'll be fun to go to the poetry night," said Carolyn.

"Poetry slam," said Maya, correcting her. "What are you going to shoot?"

"I don't have an idea yet."

Joy snapped her fingers. "I got it, Carolyn. You should take pictures of the poets performing at the slam. You took great pictures of Ivy when the Big

Bang Band performed at that street fair." She snapped her fingers again and pointed at Carolyn. "*And* it's a good way for you to get your dad to let you go. Tell him it's homework." She turned to Maya. "She could shoot at the slam, right?"

"Right," Maya agreed reluctantly. Now there was no way she could avoid bringing Carolyn and Joy to the slam.

"I'll take pictures if you will, Maya," said Carolyn.

"Sure," agreed Maya as she signaled the waiter for the check. "Why not?"

By the time Joy got home, she had only an hour to get ready for the big event at the Museum of Natural History. On the train uptown, she had debated with herself about what to wear — her new look or something dressy from her pre-Goth style. As she was showering, she thought, Carolyn's father is pretty strict. If he disapproves of how I dress, he might not want Carolyn to hang out with me. She took a pair of black satin pants and a bronze silk shirt out of the closet. I'll still wear dark red lipstick, she decided.

Her mother was working at the desk in her bedroom when Joy came in to say good-bye. She looked Joy up and down and smiled. "Well, that's *better*. I was sick of all that black. Too dark and mysterious."

I'm not sick of it, thought Joy. I *like* looking dark and mysterious. "It's just for tonight," she told her mother.

\*      \*      \*

Carolyn relaxed the moment she saw Joy. She had been nervous that Joy would show up in one of the weird new outfits she'd bought at Remember Me. Her father would have been sure to make a critical comment. Not to Joy's face. He had better manners than that. But she would have to hear about it later. She wondered if he noticed the little bit of gold glitter on her own eyelids.

"Both you girls look very lovely this evening," he said as he opened the door for them. "Shall we go?"

Carolyn loved nighttime events at the castlelike museum. With most of the exhibit spaces dark, the museum felt haunted. Creepy, but in a good way.

"This is a very propitious event," her father announced as they walked into the lobby. "The Hall of Ocean Life is reopened after more than a year of renovations."

A woman in a red velvet floor-length gown and a man in a tuxedo passed them. Joy and Carolyn exchanged a look. "This *is* fancy," Carolyn whispered. She was glad she'd worn her green silk dress. "Sunday best," her grandfather would say.

"Do they still have that huge model of a whale in the Hall of Ocean Life?" Joy asked Mr. Kuhlberg. "It looked so real."

"Well, you'll be happy to hear that we do, Joy," Mr. Kuhlberg bragged as if it were *his* whale. "All ninety-four feet of it. We've done some restoration work to make it more anatomically correct."

Chattering voices and bright live music wafted

toward them. Mr. Kuhlberg stepped back for the girls to enter ahead of him.

They walked onto the second-story balcony of a two-story hall. Carolyn didn't know where to look first — up at the humongous gray model whale hanging from the ceiling or down into the crowded first floor. The arched whale seemed to be swimming toward them. Huge vases of apple blossoms and lilacs on stands that looked like sea coral reached toward them on the second floor. Below her — under the suspended whale — men and women talked and took drinks and hors d'oeuvres from passing waiters in white jackets.

"This is great!" exclaimed Joy. "I didn't know it would be so formal and that there'd be so many people." And they're not all *old*, she thought as she noticed a cute guy under the whale.

"My dad will introduce us to some of them," Carolyn told Joy as they walked down the stairs behind him. "He is *always* introducing me to people at these things. And because it's a museum, he tries to make it educational. You'll see."

Carolyn's father reached the bottom of the staircase and turned to them. "Girls, let me introduce you to Dr. Gerald Granger." A white-haired gentleman smiled up at the girls as they descended the last two steps. "Dr. Granger, this is my daughter, Carolyn, and her friend Joy Benoit-Cohen. Dr. Granger has been very involved in the renovation of the Hall of Ocean Life.

He is head of mammals — which, of course, includes whales."

Carolyn nudged Joy with her elbow before saying, "Nice to meet you, Dr. Granger."

Joy coughed away her laugh before adding, "The whale looks so real."

Carolyn noticed that the room was ringed with dioramas of sea creatures. "Can we go off on our own, Dad?" she asked. "We want to look at the exhibits."

Joy arched an eyebrow in Carolyn's direction before saying, "The exhibits look very educational."

"Indeed they are," agreed Mr. Kuhlberg. He looked at his watch. "It's seven-thirty. Meet me at the Walrus exhibit in half an hour."

The girls moved into the crowd. "Is your dad a doctor, too?" Joy asked Carolyn. "Like *Doctor* Granger."

Carolyn nodded. "He's a doctor of Entomology. But he doesn't care if you call him doctor or not."

"As long as the cockroaches know," said Joy.

"Right," agreed Carolyn.

They took miniature quiches and cocktail napkins from a passing waiter. "Let's get something to drink," suggested Joy.

Carolyn pointed at the underbelly of the whale and the ceiling, rippling blue and white above. "It feels like we're in the ocean underneath a whale," she exclaimed.

Joy looked up. "A party at the bottom of the sea."

They both got cranberry juice and ginger ale cocktails from the bar.

"We have to look at some of the exhibits before we go back to your dad," Joy reminded Carolyn.

"Yes," agreed Carolyn. "Let's work our way around to the walruses."

They started with the sea lions.

"They look so real," commented Joy. "It's like they're looking back at us."

"They'd be surprised to see you standing there staring at them," said a male voice. Carolyn turned to see a *very* cute guy. Joy recognized him as the guy she'd noticed before. His name tag read, JEFF KAPLAN, INTERN.

"I guess they *would* be surprised," agreed Carolyn. As the words came out, she wanted to take them back. It was such a lame thing to say. A blush rose up her cheeks. Why did cute guys make her shy?

Jeff Kaplan, intern, looked up at the whale. "Pretty impressive, isn't it?"

"It is," agreed Joy. "It's so *big*." It was her turn to think, That was a lame thing to say.

Jeff Kaplan introduced himself and said that he was a junior in marine biology at the University of Massachusetts.

They said who they were but didn't say that they were in *junior* high.

"If you want, I'll look at the exhibits with you," Jeff offered. "I know all about them."

Is he showing us around because it's his intern

job? Carolyn wondered as they followed him to the next exhibit. Or is he doing it because he wants to?

Jeff was smart.

Jeff was cool.

Jeff asked them what they were going to do after they graduated from high school.

"I'm interested in horses," answered Carolyn. "I've thought about working in one of the wild horse rescue programs in Wyoming."

"I'm going to be a photographer," said Joy, surprising herself with her own answer. Well, it sounded good. Maybe she would be a photographer.

Jeff was telling them that whales ate giant octopuses when Carolyn's father came up to them. A pretty woman with pulled-back black hair and bright red lipstick was by his side.

"Carolyn," said her father. "I'd like you to meet a colleague, Dr. Maxine Geng. Dr. Geng is a professor of entomology at Columbia." He turned to Joy. "And this is Carolyn's friend Joy Benoit-Cohen."

As Joy and Maxine shook hands, Carolyn stared at the name tag pinned to Dr. Geng's gold-colored top. DR. MAXINE GENG, it announced. M. G.? She's Dad's girlfriend! The one he buys flowers for. The one who calls him "darling."

Dr. Geng took Carolyn's hand. "Your father has told me so much about you, Carolyn."

"All good," he said with a big smile in Maxine's direction.

Carolyn said, "Nice to meet you, Dr. Geng." But

she didn't mean it. She turned to her father. "We didn't get to see all the exhibits. Can we?"

"Children who are interested in marine biology," said Dr. Geng. "How encouraging."

"Can we, Dad?" Carolyn repeated, not looking at her.

"See you back here in an hour then," he agreed.

He's probably glad to be rid of me, Carolyn thought as she led Joy away. He wants to be alone with Dr. Geng. With M.G.

Carolyn had forgotten all about Jeff. But Joy hadn't. He had disappeared with a nod to her when Mr. Kuhlberg began the introductions. As she followed Carolyn through the crowd, she looked around for him. When they reached the bar, she caught his eye across the room. Or had he caught hers? He smiled, gave a little wave, and disappeared into the crowd again.

Carolyn was drinking her soda and eyeing a passing tray of itty-bitty brownies when the dancing started. Thoughts about her dad and Maxine Geng kept going through her head — even when she was talking to Joy about how good the brownies were, how cute Jeff was, and how funny some people looked dancing. How could she get the idea of her dad and Maxine out of her head? As the music revved up into a fast number, she turned to Joy and said, "Let's dance."

But dancing didn't solve the problem. Not even when Jeff danced with them. How could she forget her dad and M. G. when, just across the dance floor, they were dancing — with each other.

Sunday, Joy went downtown to babysit for Jake while her father and Sue went to the movies. When her baby half brother saw her, he happily shouted, "Oy! Oy!"

Her father raised his voice, too — but not happily. "What are you wearing?"

"Just clothes," she answered. She'd forgotten that he hadn't seen her dressed Goth. "I'm trying a new look."

"Well, I don't like it."

Jake was in her arms now, playing with a silver skull hanging from her black vinyl choker.

"Does your boyfriend dress like that?" asked Sue.

"I don't have a boyfriend," Joy said.

"No wonder," her father muttered.

"So that's why you're dressing like that," said Sue, satisfied. "Because you're upset about the break-up with your boyfriend."

"Well, just be sure you don't dress that way when we go to dinner next Saturday," her father was saying. "We might see someone I know."

Dinner with her dad next Saturday? When she had dinner with her father, it was always on Fridays. Now she remembered that he'd asked to change it to Saturday because of some Friday thing he had to do with Sue.

"But I'm busy on Saturday," she told him, glad that she was. Who wanted to have dinner with him, anyway?

"A date?" asked Sue.

Joy wiggled her black nails for Jake to see. Delighted, he grabbed two of them. "It's not a date. I'm going to a poetry slam thing with my friends. Maya invited me."

"Cool," said Sue.

"Where is it?" asked her father.

"Near Maya's. At some community center. In a church."

"Aren't you spending a lot of time in Harlem?" her father asked.

"I guess." She put Jake down and he toddled over to a pile of children's books.

"I'd prefer you didn't."

"What's wrong with Harlem?" Joy asked. A new thought ran across her mind. Was her father racist?

"It can be dangerous in Harlem," Sue answered for him.

"You have your own neighborhoods," added her father. "You live in two of the best neighborhoods in the New York. Where are the Upper East Side kids you grew up with? They're the ones you should be hanging out with. And you have downtown. Most city kids would love to hang out down here. It's where it's happening."

He sounds like such a jerk, Joy thought. A racist jerk. My dad! I hate this. "One of my best friends lives in Harlem," she told him. "So I go up there sometimes. And, in case you didn't know, Harlem is happening, too."

Sue looked from her husband to her stepdaughter and put up her hands. "Okay, you two," she said with a nervous giggle. "Cease-fire."

Jake was back, pulling on his sister's skirt and holding up a book. "Ook. Ook," he shouted.

Later, while she played blocks with Jake, she remembered how her mother was always saying her father was a snob. Well, she thought, maybe Mom's right. The fight with her dad was still on her mind when Jake fell asleep in her arms.

As she put him in the crib, she thought, I told Dad that Maya is one of my best friends. If she is, I can call her now, just to talk. Friends do that. I'll tell her about the party at the museum and the cute guy we met.

As Joy speed-dialed Maya's number she thought, She probably isn't even there. She's probably doing something with Carolyn.

But Maya *was* there. And she was alone — cleaning her room. When the portable phone rang, she put a pile of dirty clothes back on her bed and answered it. Maybe it was Shana. They'd all had so much fun at Delores's birthday party last night. Maybe they could be best friends again.

It wasn't Shana. It was Joy. Joy who was, for a change, sounding kind of — joyful. She described the party she'd gone to at the museum with Carolyn. The party that Carolyn had invited Maya to first. She was going on about some older guy they met and how they'd danced with him. Then she asked, "What did you do last night?"

"I went to a party at Delores's," answered Maya. "For her birthday. It was fun. Alex was there — with Shana."

Would I have had even more fun at that party? wondered Joy. Well, I wasn't invited, so it doesn't make any difference. "Was Serge there?" she asked.

"No," answered Maya.

"But he and Alex are such good friends," protested Joy. "Maybe he didn't go because Alex and Shana were, like, on a date."

Maya picked a sock up off the floor. "Or maybe Serge had something else to do." She pictured the kids at the party. Every one of them was black.

After Maya hung up, she thought, The real reason Serge — or Carolyn or Joy — wasn't invited was because they are white. She didn't tell Joy that.

And she didn't tell Joy that she and Shana got along great for the first time in a long time. Or that Shana was going to be performing in the poetry slam they were all going to on Saturday.

# Abyssinian Baptist Church

The first thing that Carolyn noticed about the group of kids outside the Abyssinian Baptist Church was that most of them were black. The slightly scared, outsider feeling she had when she first moved to New York City crept over her again.

When Maya saw the crowd, she thought, Everyone's going to hang around outside until just before the slam starts. She gave Joy's sleeve a little tug. "Let's go in."

"Hey, Maya, wait up!" a voice called out. She turned and saw Jay-Cee running toward them. Good, she thought. It's not just me with two white girls.

"You stuck to the Goth," Jay-Cee told Joy when she reached them. "It looks so great on you. Could go darker with the lipstick though." Her smile included Carolyn now. "So you all came out to hear Shana perform."

Joy and Carolyn exchanged a look that said, Maya didn't tell us Shana was in the slam.

"Alex is coming to hear her, too," Jay-Cee said as they filed into the hall. "And Serge. We're supposed to save them seats."

"Where's Delores?" asked Carolyn.

"With Loreen and that crowd," answered Jay-Cee.

Maya rolled her eyes. *Neither of us liked Loreen*, thought Maya, *and Loreen has never liked me.*

Joy looked around the room, hoping to find Serge. He'd be easy to spot, with his bleached hair.

Meanwhile, Carolyn asked Jay-Cee, "What's Shana's poem about?"

Jay-Cee shrugged. "Don't know. Didn't even know she was on a team." She gave Maya's camera bag a tug. "You must have known."

"She got into it when she worked at that day camp last summer," Maya explained. "It was a workshop thing for the counselors-in-training. You know, after the little kids went home. I guess she was so good she got on a team."

"She always liked to do rhymes," commented Jay-Cee. "What's that one she did for jump rope when we were little?"

"Touch Your Knee," remembered Maya.

"That's it," Jay-Cee agreed. She began the jump rope rhyme. *"One, two, three . . . touch your knee."*

Maya joined in. *"With one more . . . we have four. . . . Five, six, seven . . . reach for heaven. . . . Eight, nine, ten . . . let's start again."*

"That's great," laughed Carolyn.

"How old was Shana when she made that up?" Joy asked.

"We were in the second grade," remembered

Maya. She led her group toward the front of the hall. If they were going to take pictures, they should be close to the stage.

Joy scanned the crowd for Serge again. She still didn't see him. They filed into an empty row of seats. Joy laid her scarf over the two seats next to her and told Carolyn, "We'll save these seats for Serge and Alex."

The MC — Zakia — ran onto the stage. Carolyn loved Zakia's look. Long dreadlocks, loose jeans, and a tight bright orange T-shirt. She had a big smile and welcomed everyone.

Joy thought that Zakia looked great, too. But mostly she was impressed with how quickly and well she explained the rules for a slam. When she said that the judges were scattered throughout the audience, they stood and held up their piles of scoring cards — each with a number from 1 to 10.

"Booing is all right," Zakia concluded. She slowed down her patter to add, "But puh-lease don't abuse our poor judges."

Everyone laughed.

"Now, welcome to the stage our first poet of the evening. "T-y-y!"

As Ty ran onto the stage, Alex and Serge came up the aisle. Serge sat next to Joy. He looked down the row of girls, grinned, and waved.

Meanwhile, Ty broke into his poem. "What's Your Beef?" It was a fast-talking poem about working at a fast-food restaurant.

Ty left the stage with a score of seven, a few boos, and a lot of applause.

"He talks too fast for me," Serge whispered to Joy.

"Sorry," Joy whispered back. Poor Serge, she thought. Slam poets almost always talk fast.

Maya leaned toward Carolyn and whispered, "Let's take some pictures."

They went to the side aisle where they wouldn't block anyone's view of the stage. Carolyn felt self-conscious and half wished she hadn't agreed to take pictures.

Michele — the next poet — came onto the stage. Carolyn took a shot.

*Michele grinning out at the crowd. Click.*

"This is not another poetry bummer," Michele began. "It's a happy poem about summer."

Maya moved in for a close-up.

*Michele holding up the fingers of one hand as she lists great things about summer. Click.*

Carolyn got the shot of Michele saying her last line, "I think people are dumber in the summer. Now *that's* a bummer."

Carolyn forgot all about being self-conscious.

*Michele bowing. Click.*

Michele got two points and a lot of boos.

Shana was next.

Carolyn looked through her lens as Shana ran out onstage.

*Shana mouthing, "Don't!" to the camera.*

Carolyn didn't take the shot. As she lowered her camera she saw that Maya was still looking through her lens.

*Shana glaring. Click.*

In the instant that Maya took the picture, she realized Shana was glaring at her and was mouthing, "Don't," meaning "Don't take my picture." Maya lowered her camera, too.

Shana shouted the first part of her poem at the audience:

> "Stop. Don't. Get out of my way.
> You're no good. Do what I say."

She moved a step sideways, looked at where she'd just stood, and answered the angry voice of the first part of the poem:

> "Uh-huh. Yep. Okay.
> I'm trying, Ma.
> But why you gotta be this way?"

Joy stopped worrying about whether Serge could keep up with the fast talk of slam poetry. She was concentrating completely on Shana's poem.

Shana narrowed her eyes and leaned toward the audience and went back to the yelling voice:

> "You got some problems with me, child?
> It frighten you 'cause I'm wild?

*You're just a stupid kid who don't even*
   *know what life's about —*
*Leave me alone. Let me sleep. Go on out."*

Maya couldn't take her eyes off Shana as she went through the next two stanzas. It was clear to Maya that Shana had written the poem about herself. It was her mother who yelled and called her stupid. How awful.

Before the last stanza, Shana paused and looked at the audience with a wide-eyed innocent look:

*"All I did*
*Was be her kid.*
*I don't know no other*
*mother.*
*So tell me true,*
*Is the color of mother love black and*
   *blue?"*

She leaned closer to the mike.
The hall was dead silent.
Shana whispered her last line in a husky voice:

*"I'm black. And I'm blue. How about you?"*

The crowd clapped and stamped. No one booed.
I'm not black, thought Joy. But I'm blue — a lot of the time.

As Maya clapped, she swallowed back a lump

moving up her throat. My best friend, black and blue, she thought. Shana just told us her mother hit her. Why didn't I know that?

As soon as Carolyn got up on Sunday morning, she called Joy. She wanted to make sure their plan for the day was still on. She was afraid if she wasn't busy, her father would invite her to do something that included M. G.

Since Carolyn met M. G. at the museum, her father had been dropping Dr. Geng's name into their conversations.

On Wednesday morning: "I'm attending a lecture at Columbia this afternoon. Dr. Geng is speaking. You met her at the museum."

Thursday morning: "Dr. Geng's lecture was excellent. She is a very intelligent woman. I was quite impressed."

Saturday morning: "Since you're going to that poetry event tonight, I think I'll go to the movies." She didn't need to hear Dr. Geng's name to know *who* he'd be going to the movies with.

As she handed him the frying pan for their Sunday morning eggs, she thought, Dad used to go to the good movies with me.

During breakfast, she told him all about the poetry slam, except for the fact that the audience booed poems they didn't like. Her father wouldn't understand that part. He'd call it bad manners. But she hadn't minded. The poets didn't seem to, either.

"Do you have plans today?" he asked.

She put a smear of cream cheese on the last of her bagel. "Joy and I are going to the park to take pictures." She glanced out the window at the blue sky. It was a good day to take pictures. "You said yesterday I could."

"Did I?" he said absentmindedly. "I forgot."

He never used to forget my schedule, she thought.

The phone rang.

She jumped down from the stool. "I'll get it."

It was Joy. "Should I call Maya and see if she wants to go to the park, too?"

"You could ask her," Carolyn told Joy.

After she hung up, Carolyn remembered how odd Maya had acted at the slam. During intermission and after the performance, Maya'd left her and Joy to talk to neighborhood friends. When they followed her, Maya didn't even introduce them. Will Maya *want* to hang out with us? she wondered.

Joy speed-dialed Maya. On the third ring she thought, Maya's probably busy with her uptown friends.

Maya saw on caller ID that the call was from Joy. If she wants me to do something, she thought, I can't. Today Jay-Cee, Shana, and I are painting and decorating Delores's bedroom. It was their IOU birthday present to Delores. Maya was glad she had something to do in her own neighborhood with other black girls. It was a good excuse not to hang out with Carolyn and Joy.

She answered the phone on the fourth ring.

As Carolyn walked out of her building to meet Joy, she saw Ivy — dog-walker and drummer — coming toward her with Precious, the largest dog Carolyn had ever seen. Carolyn had photographed Ivy walking dogs and performing with her band, the Big Bang Band, at a street fair. She'd even taken pictures of Ivy's small all-blue apartment, which had a bathtub in the kitchen and a view of an old cemetery. Carolyn's father had taken Carolyn and her friends to a concert at the Cathedral of St. John the Divine where Ivy drummed on a metal tree of hanging pots, pans, and bells. Ivy's great, thought Carolyn.

Ivy grinned when she saw Carolyn. "Hey, Red, what's up?"

"Going to the park with Joy," answered Carolyn. "She's going to take pictures. What's up with you?"

"Jammed all night with some friends at an after-hours club," she answered. "I'm beat." She grinned again. "But it was worth it."

Precious sniffed Carolyn's hand before going into the building with Ivy.

I want to be like Ivy, Carolyn thought as she ran toward the park. Independent and fun, but still sort of spiritual. Ivy believes her ancestors' spirits live on in her. I hope I have my mother's spirit in me.

Joy was waiting for her at the West 81st Street entrance to the park. They walked slowly along the path. "So what do you want to shoot?" Carolyn asked.

Joy noticed a paper bag lying in the grass. "Inanimate things like that bag." She aimed her camera at it.

*Close-up of crumbled brown bag in the grass. Click.*

Carolyn heard a familiar sound. Like a horse's whinny. In New York? she thought. I must have imagined it.

The sound again. This time louder.

"Is that a horse?" asked Joy.

An alarm sounded inside Carolyn. It was a horse. A horse in trouble. She could tell by the whinny. She stepped up on a bench and looked all around. Uptown, between tree branches, she spotted the flash of a golden mane.

She jumped down from the bench and ran north.

"What's going on?" Joy called as she ran after her.

Carolyn didn't answer. All her energy was already focused on the horse. She ran around the children's playground toward the sound.

The whinny again. Closer. Frightened and fierce.

On the other side of the playground, she saw him. Golden coat and mane. Rearing up. Eyes wild with fear.

Three men in running clothes surrounded him — all shouting at once.

"Get him."

"Where's the rider?"

"Someone's going to get hurt."

The horse, shiny with sweat, reared up again and pawed the air. One of the men picked up a stick and swung it at the horse like a knight facing a dragon.

"Back off," Carolyn ordered the man in a firm voice.

He swung the stick again.

"Now!" she insisted.

"I think she knows what to do," Joy told him. "She grew up with horses."

The jogger put the stick down and backed away.

Carolyn walked slowly toward the horse.

Joy looked through the lens of her camera.

*Carolyn standing still. Horse rearing. Click.*

# Claremont Stables

Carolyn stood still with her hands by her side, looked straight at the horse, and sent out strong, clear thoughts. *You're going to be okay. I am not afraid. I can help. I will take care of you. Trust me.*

Finally, the horse noticed her and met her gaze. Still frightened, he pawed the ground. But he kept glancing back to Carolyn.

She didn't move. "It's all right," she said in a calm voice. "Everything is going to be all right."

"Be careful. He's wild," the jogger who'd waved the stick yelled.

The horse looked around frantically and whinnied.

"Come on, boy, come to me," she repeated.

Joy shot the man an angry look and mouthed, "Be quiet!"

The man glared back at her, but he stopped shouting.

"It's all right," Carolyn reassured the horse in a super-calm voice. "Come on. Come on. Come to me."

*The horse taking a step toward Carolyn. Click.*

*The horse lowering his head in front of Carolyn. Click.*

*Carolyn and the horse. Carolyn holding him by the reins. Click.*

"What are you going to do with him?" the runner with the stick asked.

The horse jerked his head toward the man and rolled his eyes fearfully. Carolyn held on to the reins with one hand and stroked his neck with the other. "It's okay. It's okay."

"You can go," Joy told the man. "We've got the situation under control." She spotted a man in riding clothes limping along the bridle path toward them. "And there's the rider."

"Come on, George," one of the other runners urged. "We got four more miles."

Carolyn didn't look at the runners or Joy going to meet the rider. She kept her focus on the horse.

Joy reached the injured rider and told him, "My friend caught your horse. Are you okay?"

"Yes. Fine. Thank you." He stood straighter. "Thank you for rescuing Maximillian. I'm Fredrick Lewis."

Fredrick Lewis had dirt all over his side, a smudge on his cheek, and was limping. He'd lost his horse. But he hadn't lost his manners.

Joy nodded and smiled. "How do you do, Mr. Lewis. I'm Joy. My friend, Carolyn, is the one who calmed down your horse. Maximillian." She took out her cell phone. "Do you want me to call an ambulance for you."

"Oh, no," he protested. "I'm all right. Quite all right. Just a bruise to the knee. I'm a medical doctor, so I know about these things. A little ice and rest and I'll be fine. I want to check on Maximillian, however."

A soft whinny came from behind Joy. She turned.

*Carolyn leading the calmed horse toward his owner. Click.*

Dr. Lewis thanked Carolyn and patted his horse's neck. "I don't know what spooked him," he said. "Maximillian is used to the city and the bridle path. We've been riding here for five years."

Carolyn pointed to a spot on Max's hindquarter. "Maybe he was stung by a wasp or something."

Dr. Lewis studied the spot. "That would make anyone jump," he agreed. "Man or horse."

Carolyn ran a hand along Maximillian's silken side and asked, "Where do you keep him?"

"At the Claremont Stables on 89th Street."

"On the West Side?" asked Carolyn, surprised.

He nodded and rubbed his own bruised leg. "Where are we now? I've gotten all turned around by this fall."

"Near 88th Street," answered Joy.

"Carolyn, you seem to be good with horses," Dr. Lewis observed.

"I grew up on a horse ranch in Wyoming," she explained. "I've been around horses all my life."

"I'm wondering if you wouldn't mind taking Maximillian back to Claremont for me?" Dr. Lewis asked. "I would be very grateful."

Carolyn put her hand on the horse's strong neck. His pulse rate wasn't racing anymore. "I would like to."

"I'll take a cab," Dr. Lewis said, "and meet you there."

He limped toward Central Park West with Joy and Carolyn. Dr. Lewis hailed a cab, and Carolyn led Maximilian across Central Park West.

"Did you know about these stables?" Carolyn asked Joy as they walked down 89th Street.

"I took lessons there when I was little, but I quit after a couple of weeks." Should I tell Carolyn how frightened I was being up on such a big animal? Joy wondered.

"Were you scared?" asked Carolyn. "It can be pretty scary when you first start riding."

"Yeah. I was. And the kids in my riding group were really snotty. They were all these skinny little things. I heard them whispering about me. One said, "'She'll probably break the horse's back.'" Joy looked at the ground. She'd never told anyone that. The memory of it still hurt.

"That's awful," sympathized Carolyn. "No wonder you quit."

Maximillian nodded as if to agree.

Dr. Lewis's cab was waiting for them at 89th Street and Columbus Avenue. He leaned out of the cab and pointed down the block. "Claremont is toward the end, on the right."

As the two girls and horse continued down 89th Street, Carolyn listened to the even *clip-clop clip-clop* of Maximillian's hooves on the pavement.

A mother pushing a stroller of twins in the other direction smiled at Carolyn. "Horsey," Carolyn heard the woman tell her children. "Big horsey goes *neigh, neigh.*"

Dr. Lewis and a groom were waiting for them in front of an old four-story stone building below a sign reading CLAREMONT STABLES.

The groom took the reins from Carolyn. She gave Maximillian a final pat and wished him a silent good-bye. She wondered what his life was like inside the building.

"Are a lot of horses boarded here?" she asked Dr. Lewis.

"A hundred or so," he answered. "They're very well cared for."

They may be well cared for, thought Carolyn, but there can't be that much space in there for them. City horses certainly didn't have the freedom of the horses on the ranch.

Dr. Lewis reached into his pocket for his wallet. "Let me pay you for your help and time, Carolyn."

"No," she protested. "In Wyoming, we help neighbors with their horses all the time. Especially runaways."

"Well, if there's ever anything I can do for you, here's my card." He pulled a business card from his wallet and handed it to Carolyn. "Do you have a card, then?"

Carolyn smiled at the idea of having a business card and said that she didn't.

As the two girls walked back toward Columbus Avenue, Joy said, "You were great with Maximillian. I mean you didn't act scared or anything."

"I knew that he was just frightened," Carolyn explained. "And that I could help him. I've calmed a lot of horses."

"How'd you learn to do that?" asked Joy. "It was like you were talking to him."

"In a way I was," Carolyn answered. "My mother was great with horses. I guess I inherited it from her."

Carolyn remembered when she learned she had a special way with horses. Her first pony, Jazz, was afraid to go over small wooden bridges. At first she thought the rushing water spooked him. Then she noticed he was afraid to go over a bridge that spanned a dry creek, too. One day, as she encouraged him to cross a bridge by stroking his side and talking softly to him, a picture flashed in her mind. A hoof caught in a hole in a wooden plank. Had that happened to Jazz? Carolyn told her mother her idea, and her mother spoke to the rancher who'd sold them Jazz. He said it was true. Jazz's hoof had been caught in a knothole in a bridge when he was a year old. That's when Carolyn's mother explained to her that being able to communicate with horses was a special talent and not something everyone could do. "And you have the gift," she'd concluded.

Carolyn was pretty sure Joy didn't have a talent

for communicating with horses, but that didn't mean she couldn't learn to ride — and ride well.

"Maybe someday you and Maya will come out to Wyoming with me," she told Joy. "My grandpa can teach you how to ride so you won't be afraid. Riding western — out in the open — is a whole lot more fun than riding eastern in a ring. You're out in the horse's world. I think you'd like it."

"Don't you have wasps out in the open in Wyoming?" Joy asked teasingly.

"Not very big ones," Carolyn shot back. "Besides, we'd put you on old Digger. She's a thick-skinned mare. Nothing bothers her. You'll have trouble making her move."

Joy raised an eyebrow. "Sounds like fun."

Maya was having a great time decorating Delores's bedroom and being with her friends. First, they cleared everything off the walls, put the furniture in the middle of the room, and covered it with an old sheet. Next, Shana and Delores painted the walls and trim a light orange. Maya painted the bureau and a nightstand aqua. Meanwhile, Jay-Cee went to Remember Me to finish sewing up a bedcover and curtains from a lime green, aqua, and pink floral fabric Mrs. Johnson had donated to the makeover project. After they put up the new curtains, they hung posters and arranged the furniture — all in new places. They made up the bed, puffed up the pillows, and stood back to admire their work.

"It's so Caribbean!" Delores exclaimed. "I love it."

"And so seventies," added Jay-Cee.

Maya looked around at her friends and thought, Today was perfect.

Delores bounced on the bed. "I can't wait to show Loreen."

Jay-Cee and Maya exchanged a glance. Loreen hadn't worked all day on the room. Who cared what she thought?

Later, as Maya was going up the front steps to her house, her grandmother came out from under the stoop and called, "Could you come in here a minute? I have something to show you."

Maya followed her grandmother into the ground-floor apartment. Josie took a flyer off her coffee table and handed it to Maya. "There's going to be an arts festival. For teens."

Maya studied the flyer. It was a call for poets and photographers to submit work to the Shout It/Show It Arts Festival. The show was a month away, at the Apollo Theater on 125th Street. The Apollo! thought Maya. One of the greatest theaters in New York. Maybe the world. Fabulous stars have played at the Apollo. James Brown, Richard Pryor, Billie Holiday. Gran brought me there to see Aretha Franklin. It would be amazing to show my photos at the Apollo.

She looked up at her grandmother. "Do you think I'd get in?"

Josie smiled. "It's worth a try. When I saw this, I

thought of you and your friends. You should all try out. You're all good."

"Delores and Jay-Cee don't take pictures, Gran. Or write poetry." She remembered Shana at the poetry slam. "But Shana writes poetry. She can be in the poetry part."

Josie looked at Maya quizzically. "I meant Carolyn and Joy. But you should tell Shana, too. I didn't know she wrote poetry. Good for her."

"I'm not going to invite Carolyn and Joy to do stuff with me uptown anymore, Gran," Maya explained. "And I'm not sure the Apollo's a place for my white friends. Know what I mean?"

Her grandmother sat on the arm of the couch and folded her arms. "Actually, I *don't* know what you mean. Tell me."

Maya avoided Josie's intense gaze. "My friends around the way don't like me being with white kids so much," she said to the floor. "It's a fact of life. I have to face it." She felt Josie's eyes on her. "Besides, I think that it's better that way. You know, to keep things separate."

"I don't think it is better. Are *you* two separate girls? One with white friends, the other with black friends? Besides, doesn't Jay-Cee spend time with Joy and Carolyn?"

Maya nodded. "That's the kind of person Jay-Cee is."

"You mean the kind that mixes it up? Doesn't believe in color barriers?"

Maya nodded again and poked the rug with her toe. Gran doesn't know *everything,* she thought. She doesn't know what it's like to be young in Harlem today. She met her grandmother's gaze. "That doesn't mean Jay-Cee is right. Things don't always stay the same for different generations. Maybe your generation wanted to *mix it up,* Gran, but my friends don't. So I don't. That doesn't mean I won't be friends with Joy and Carolyn. It just means that I won't be friends with them at the same time and in the same place as with my old friends. Except, I guess, Jay-Cee."

Josie stood up. "Does your father work with only black folks on the police force? Do only black people come to your mother's store?" She wagged a finger at Maya — a sure sign that she was dead-on serious. "Your school is integrated. You go all over New York City to do the things that interest you. Are you saying to Carolyn and Joy, 'I go to your neighborhood, but don't you come to mine'?"

Maya shook her head no.

"I hope not, Maya Rodriguez Johnson, because that would be plain wrong and you know it." Josie put her hand on top of Maya's head. "I think your stars must be crossed today because you are not thinking straight, girl." Josie nodded in the direction of the flyer in Maya's hand. "You, Joy, and Carolyn are good for one another. That's been clear to me from the beginning."

Sometimes they are, thought Maya. But not all the time. Not when hanging out with them makes my uptown friends angry. Not when it means nothing but trouble with my best friend.

Wednesday morning, Carolyn woke with a smile on her face. She'd been dreaming about horses — a herd of a dozen or so in different shades of brown and gray running in Central Park. The leader, an old black mare, led the herd across Sheep Meadow.

Carolyn — still only half awake — kept her eyes closed and replayed the dream in her mind's eye. The lullaby her mother used to sing her provided a sound track for her dream memory.

*"Hush-a-bye don't you cry,*
*Go to sleep-y, little baby.*
*When you wake you shall have*
*All the pretty little horses.*
*Blacks and bays, dapple grays,*
*A coach and six white horses.*
*Hush-a-bye don't you cry,*
*Go to sleep-y, little baby."*

Carolyn froze the image of the black horse mid-run. *Click.*

She opened her eyes and sat up. That's it, she thought. I have an idea for my photography project. I'll take pictures of horses in New York City.

She threw her legs over the side of the bed.

It will be so much fun.

\*　　\*　　\*

Beth opened the workshop on Saturday by passing out flyers. "There's going to be a photography exhibit and poetry performance. For teens," she explained. "The Shout It/Show It Arts Festival."

Maya took one. As she watched Carolyn and Joy read the flyer, her heart sank.

Carolyn nudged her. "This is at the Apollo. You showed us that theater."

Beth looked around the table to be sure they all had a flyer. "I encourage everyone to submit a couple of photos. There's good work coming out of this group. You should *show it*."

"Are you going to?" Carolyn whispered to Maya.

Maya pantomimed "Don't know" by shrugging her shoulders.

They took out the negatives they wanted to print and went to the darkroom. First, they exposed their negatives on printing paper. Next, they immersed the paper in developer.

Maya watched the image of Shana appear. She put it in the stop bath so it would stop printing.

Carolyn printed a negative from the poetry slam, too. It was of an Asian-American boy punching the air to emphasize the end of his poem. She liked how the boy's hand filled half of the frame, but she wanted the hand to stand out even more against the dark background. Beth helped her print the photo again. This time, when she exposed the negative onto the printing paper, she blocked the poet's hand for a few seconds. Then she developed the image. The hand was brighter than it had been in the first print. "It worked!" she told Beth excitedly.

"That's the idea," Beth said.

Charlie was at the next station. Carolyn worried that he'd have trouble in the darkroom. Is it kind of dark for him all the time? she wondered. She watched a tight close-up of a woman's face take shape in his developing bath.

He turned to her and asked, "How's my picture coming out?"

"It's looking good. Who's it of?"

"My sister. I took close-ups of everyone in my family."

Beth came up behind him. "How you doing, Charlie?"

"Not so good in the dark," he answered.

She helped him finish printing his photo.

Joy was printing her favorite shot of Carolyn with Maximillian. She did a second print, with a lighter background.

"I loved working in the darkroom!" Carolyn told Joy and Maya when they walked out of the media center together.

"Joy, I want to see that photo you took of Carolyn and the horse again," Maya said. She turned to Carolyn. "I can't believe you caught that huge horse."

"We should look at all the prints we made again," suggested Carolyn. "Let's go to the bookstore."

They headed to the mega-bookstore on Astor

Place and went up to the café on the second floor. When they were all settled with cups of hot chocolate, Joy took out a print and laid it on the table.

*Carolyn standing still in front of the terrified horse.*

"CK, you look so calm," said Maya. "What were you thinking?"

"I was thinking about him and how I would keep him safe."

"Were you, like, talking to him?" wondered Maya.

Carolyn nodded. "In my head."

"What did you say in your head?" asked Joy.

"That he should trust me. That I was in charge."

"Wow," exclaimed Maya. "That's amazing."

"It is," agreed Joy.

"It doesn't always work," commented Carolyn.

Maya turned to Joy. "It's a terrific shot. You should try out for the show at the Apollo with it." As the words came out of Maya's mouth, she regretted saying them. She had hoped the subject of the show wouldn't come up. Now she was the one who mentioned it.

"I will," agreed Joy. She pointed her finger at Carolyn. "Are you going to use the picture of that poet jabbing the air?"

Carolyn shook her head no. "I want to take pictures of horses, too," she announced. "If that's okay with you, Joy. I mean, it's sort of the same subject as yours. Only my pictures won't have any people in them."

"Fine with me," said Joy.

"Maybe we'll both get in the show, and they'll put our pictures side by side," Carolyn said enthusiastically. "That would be so cute."

"*Cute?*" said Joy with an arch of her eyebrow.

Carolyn put a hand on her hip. "Yeah, cute. You tryin' to start something?"

"Oh, I'm so-o scared," laughed Joy.

Maya didn't laugh. What if Carolyn did her bad-girl imitation in Harlem? There were kids from the neighborhood who would think she was trying to sound tough or black. Or worse, was making fun of them.

Carolyn wondered why Maya looked worried. "Can we see the print you made of Shana?" she asked.

Maya put the photo on the table. The shot was from the waist up.

*Shana, mouth tight, looking at the camera. The palm of her hand raised in a push-away gesture.*

"It's like she's trying to cover the camera lens with her hand," observed Carolyn.

"She was really angry at me," Maya explained.

"Just because you took her picture?" wondered Carolyn.

"I guess."

Joy studied the print. "To me she doesn't look angry. She looks hurt and sad." Like me sometimes, Joy thought. Sometimes people think I'm angry when I'm sad.

Carolyn studied the expression in Shana's eyes

more closely, too. "I see what you mean. Maybe she's thinking about her poem. It sounded like her mom was really awful to her."

"I didn't even know that before I heard the poem," admitted Maya. "And I was — am — her best friend."

"I wonder why she didn't tell you," said Carolyn. "I used to tell Mandy everything."

"*Everything?*" asked Joy.

"Well, *almost* everything."

"I think you can have a best friend and not tell all," said Joy. "I mean, you don't know when someone might stop being your best friend."

Like me and Shana, thought Maya as she slipped the print back into the envelope. She didn't want to talk to Carolyn and Joy about Shana anymore. "Did you ever lose a best friend?" she asked Joy.

Joy remembered Aviva Klein. "This girl Aviva and I were best friends, but she moved to California. That was the summer my parents got divorced." She didn't tell them that the day Aviva moved away was a d-a-d day so she was downtown. That she never really got to say good-bye to Aviva. That her parents were so busy being upset and angry at each other that they didn't even notice.

"How *awful*," said Carolyn. "You lost your best friend *and* your parents separated. Ugh."

Joy laughed. "It wasn't that bad."

They continued talking about friendship as they walked to the subway.

"The great thing about Mandy," Carolyn explained, "is that she's known me for as long as I can remember. We were in the same nursery school."

"Mandy knew your mother," said Maya softly.

"Yeah," agreed Carolyn. "I think, in some ways, she liked my mom better than her own mother. She was always hanging out at our place."

Maya remembered how Shana used to hang around at her house. "Shana did that, too," she said. "I guess sometimes she stayed because things were so bad at her place."

They headed down the stairs into the subway station at Eighth Street.

"We should invite Shana to do stuff with us more," suggested Carolyn. "Maybe if she gets to know Joy and me better, we could all be friends."

In your dreams, thought Joy.

"Maybe," said Maya. The roar of an approaching train sent them all running down the rest of the steps. If they hurried, they could catch that train.

They swiped their MetroCards, pushed through the turnstiles, and squeezed into a subway car.

Carolyn made room for Maya and Joy at a pole. Maya grabbed it as the train lurched forward. Carolyn — all smiles and optimism — said, "Think of something Shana likes to do, and we'll ask her."

Maya thought, Carolyn, girl, don't you know that Shana doesn't want to have anything to do with you?

# Central Park

Sunday morning, Maya woke to someone trying to open her right eyelid. She opened both eyes and saw, hovering over her, a round little face rimmed with tight curls. Her three-year-old sister, Piper.

"Are you awake, Maya?"

Maya tapped her little sister's nose with her index finger. "I am now, Miss Alarm Clock."

"I'm not a clock!" protested Piper. "I'm a girl. A big girl."

Maya pulled Piper down beside her. "If you're such a big girl, what's today?"

"Sun-day," answered Piper.

"Right!" agreed Maya. "And what happens on Sun-day?"

"You make pancakes!"

"Right again!"

"Shana, too!"

Maya brushed hair off her sister's forehead. "Shana's not coming today."

"Why?"

"She's busy."

Piper rolled closer to Maya and patted her face with her little hand. "I like Shana."

"She likes you, too, Pipe."

While Maya dressed, she thought about all the Sunday mornings she and Shana had made pancakes for her younger sisters. It started when Maya and Shana were ten and Josie taught them how. On one of those pancake-Sundays, Maya had noticed black-and-blue marks on Shana's arms. Shana had worn a long-sleeved shirt that day. But she had rolled up the sleeves to do dishes,

Maya saw the bruises on her arm and asked, "What happened?"

Shana quickly rolled her sleeves back down. "I fell. In the hall of my building."

"How?" Maya asked.

"Slipped on a banana peel," Shana answered with a laugh. "Just like in the jokes."

But Shana's bruises weren't a joke. They were, Maya thought, what Shana was talking about in the poem she performed at the slam.

Maya poured milk into the pancake mix and stirred. Why didn't Shana tell me her mother hit her? she wondered. Did she think I knew? A third question popped into her mind. If Shana thought I knew, didn't she wonder why I never talked to her about it?

"Maya, the pancakes got bubbles," Piper shouted. "Plip them. Plip them."

Maya looked down at the silver-dollar pancakes on the griddle. Piper — with her bird's-eye view from a perch on the counter — was right. "You *flip* pan-cakes, Pipe," she said as she did it. "Not *plip*."

"Shana says *plip*," observed Piper.

Maya laughed. "Don't you know she was just playin' with you?"

"Shana made me a Barney pancake," Piper said. "I *ate* Barney."

"I know." Maya remembered in a rush the different-shaped pancakes Shana had come up with for the girls — flowers, dinosaurs, hearts.

Maya pointed the spatula at Piper. "Go tell Han-nah and Naomi that the first batch is ready."

After pancakes, Maya headed out alone to take pictures for her workshop project. She hoped that something she took would be good enough for the arts festival.

As she wandered from street to street, she shot buildings and street scenes. She was putting in a sec-ond roll of film when she noticed that she was across the street from Shana's building. The building was run-down. Half the windows were boarded up with sheet metal. Her father had told her not to go there. "Shana can come here anytime," he'd said, "but I don't want you going to her place."

Well, I didn't plan to come here, Maya thought. I just ended up on Shana's block. It must be a sign that I should find Shana and talk to her. I'll ask her about those bruises I saw on her arm that Sunday. I'll tell her I'm sorry that I didn't know about the trouble she was having at home.

She crossed the street to Shana's building. The lock on the front door was broken. She went in and started up the six flights of stairs to Shana's apartment.

The stairwell and halls were dark and smelled of urine. Between the fourth and fifth floors, a tough-looking guy passed her going down. *If he threatens me, I could hit him with my camera,* passed through her head. That thought was swiftly followed by, *If he doesn't steal it first.*

Maya kept going up and the man kept going down. When she glanced over her shoulder, he was looking over his shoulder at her.

She ran the last flight of stairs and pressed the buzzer for apartment 6F. No one came to the door.

She knocked. Still no answer.

Shana wasn't home.

Maya pulled the arts festival flyer out of her pocket and dug around in her grandfather's camera bag for a pen. The one she found read METROPOLITAN TRANSIT AUTHORITY along the side. It was her grandfather's pen from when he was a bus driver. She used it to write a note on the back of the flyer. SHANA, I CAME BY TO TALK TO YOU. CALL ME. MAYA. P.S. I HOPE YOU'LL DO A POEM FOR THE SHOUT IT/SHOW IT FESTIVAL. SEE OTHER SIDE OF THIS NOTE. M.

As Maya slipped the note under Shana's door, she remembered the guy on the stairs. Was he waiting for her in the hall? Outside? She was afraid to leave and afraid to stay. Was this what it was like for Shana every day? she wondered.

Maya rushed down the stairs and pushed open the front door.

*Slow down,* she scolded herself. *Don't act afraid.*

A couple of guys were sitting on the stoop of a boarded-up building across the street. Some little kids playing tag ran down the street.

Maya continued to coach herself. *Be calm. Walk with confidence. Don't run.*

She looked to her right and left.

No sign of Scary Guy.

As she walked down the street, she noticed the sun lighting up the end of the block in a golden glow. She snapped the lens cap off her camera and sighted a long shot down the block.

She was taking a second shot when a voice growled in her ear, "Gimme the camera." Something poked her in the back. A gun?

Maya froze. *Should I give him the camera? Or try to hit him with it? Should I beg him not to hurt me? Will he hurt me anyway?*

Laughter. Shana's laughter.

Maya spun around.

"Shana!" she screamed. "Are you crazy? I could have hurt you!"

"I'm the one with the gun," teased Shana, holding up the two fingers she'd poked in Maya's back.

"It's *not* funny! You really scared me."

"What are you doing here, anyway?" asked Shana. "Taking pictures of the slums to show your new downtown friends?"

"Stop it!" Maya shouted angrily. "Why are you being like this? What kind of a friend are you?"

Shana glared and shouted back, "What kind of a friend am I? You got some kind of a short memory to ask me that, girl. What kind of friend you think you've been to *me* lately?"

"A better one than you," Maya shot back.

"I gotta go, Oreo," Shana hissed. She turned and walked away.

*Oreo,* Maya thought. Black on the outside, but white on the inside. How dare Shana call me an Oreo! How dare she scare me like that!

"Shana, come back here!" Maya shouted after Shana.

But it was too late. Shana was gone. Into her building.

On Wednesday, Carolyn and Maya's school let out at noon for a teachers' conference. "Want to do something this afternoon?" Maya asked as they left school together.

"Okay," agreed Carolyn, "but I have to call my dad. I forgot to tell him I had the afternoon off." She took the cell phone out of her pocket. "What're we going to do? I'll have to tell him that, too."

Maya looked up at the clear blue sky. It had been a cold, snowy winter, and spring was late getting started. But today was sunny and the warmest it had been in weeks. A perfect day to have the afternoon off from school. "Let's go to the park."

"Can we go to where they line up the carriage horses?" asked Carolyn. "I want to take pictures of the horses."

"Let's do it," agreed Maya.

While they walked to the subway, Carolyn dialed her father's office number. "You have reached Dr. Kuhlberg's office," his recorded voice announced. "I am out of the office or on the other line. Please leave a message."

She did.

Half an hour later, Carolyn was scanning a lineup of five carriage horses and their drivers.

"That white horse in the front is pretty," observed Maya.

Carolyn shook her head. "I'm looking for the Belgian horse that Jay-Cee posed with. You know, when Joy took her modeling pictures." As Carolyn was saying this to Maya, she spotted the Belgian in the fourth position.

When they reached the horse, the driver — dressed in a tuxedo — tipped a top hat in their direction. "Ride, girls?" he asked.

When Carolyn explained that she wanted to photograph his horse, the driver remembered them. "You were with that model and the girl taking her picture."

"Right," agreed Maya.

Carolyn was already standing in front of the horse, silently communicating with him.

"What's his name?" Carolyn asked.

"Jolly," answered the man. "He's a good horse." He jiggled the reins. "You're jolly, aren't you, Jolly?"

But Jolly — Carolyn saw and felt — wasn't jolly today. He was tired and sore. She stepped back and looked up and down the line of carriages and focused on the other horses. None of them looked happy to her.

"Where do these horses go at night?" she asked Jolly's driver.

The driver jumped down from his carriage and spoke in a low voice. "Between you and me, to a not-very-good stable. Jolly just got moved there last month. The other place was better, but it got sold to real estate developers. Now he's on the top floor of a building with very small stalls."

"Oh," said Carolyn. "Are the horses ever free to graze or just run?"

He shook his head. "I do the best I can by Jolly. I'm hoping to find a place to retire him next year. Upstate some place." He looked up and down the line of carriages and lowered his voice even more. "But for most of these poor beasts it's" — he hesitated before completing the sentence — "the slaughterhouse."

Jolly turned his head and looked at Carolyn. She raised her camera.

*Jolly, sadness showing in his eyes. Click.*

*Long shot of horse and carriage from the side. Click.*

"How about a short ride, girls?" the driver asked. "On the house." He patted Jolly affectionately on the neck. "Jolly won't mind." He pointed his riding crop toward the carriage in front of them. Four large adults were climbing aboard. "You'll be easier for Jolly to take around than them. Besides, he likes the park."

Maya and Carolyn looked at each other. "You could get some great moving shots," Maya observed.

Carolyn turned to Jolly. Maybe the driver was right. Maybe Jolly would rather be walking through the park than standing idly in line. She climbed into the carriage.

The driver directed Jolly to turn and they *clop-clopped* into Central Park.

*Shot from carriage of Jolly's neck and blowing mane. Click.*

Carolyn leaned over the edge to get a side view.

*Jolly's smart step. Click.*

*Close-up of Jolly's head, mane, and ears from above. Click.*

"There are lots of people out today," commented Maya.

Carolyn looked around and saw that Maya was right. Mothers and nannies pushing strollers, people on benches reading papers and eating take-out lunches, couples walking hand in hand. She sighted one couple through the camera and zoomed in for a closer look. "It's like having binoculars," she commented to Maya. She panned to another couple walking hand in hand and dropped the camera to her lap. It was her dad and M. G.! At that instant, he looked up and she saw him see her. She looked away.

"Isn't that your dad?" Maya whispered.

"Yes."

The driver was turning the carriage around. "You get enough shots, miss?"

"Yes," Carolyn answered. "Thank you. I'm finished."

As Jolly pulled the carriage back the way they came, Maya asked Carolyn, "Is that your father's girlfriend?"

Carolyn looked down at her lap. "I guess. I met her. She's a doctor. Of entomology. Bugs. Like him."

This is really upsetting Carolyn, thought Maya. I can see it. "I'm sorry," she said softly.

Jolly's driver turned to them. "Want to hear my spiel about the Central Park Zoo?" he asked.

"Sure," said Carolyn.

For the rest of the ride, he talked about the history of the Central Park Zoo and listed all the different animals that lived there, including red pandas, sea lions, penguins, tamarin monkeys, polar bears, and poison tree frogs.

I hope the animals in the zoo have a better life than Jolly, Carolyn thought as she climbed out of the carriage.

The two girls walked slowly up Fifth Avenue.

Maya expected Carolyn to talk about seeing her father and his girlfriend. She didn't.

For the first five blocks, Carolyn talked about the

difficult life of a carriage horse in New York City and what should be done about it.

For the next five blocks she talked about the difficult life of some horses in the wild and what should be done about it.

As Carolyn spun out all these complaints for horses, in the back of her mind she was thinking: I saw my father and M. G. together. I saw them holding hands. And he saw me see them.

Maya knew that Carolyn was talking about horses to try to forget what was really on her mind. I won't bring up the subject of Carolyn's father, she decided, unless she does.

"Hey, we're near Joy's," Carolyn announced after another few blocks.

"Let's call her cell and see if she wants to meet us," suggested Maya. "Or do you have to go home?"

"Not yet," Carolyn answered. She pulled the cell phone out of her jacket pocket, dialed Joy's number, and handed the phone to Maya.

Joy was halfway home from school when her phone rang.

When she heard Maya's voice, she exclaimed happily, "Hi! What's up?"

"We're on Seventy-ninth and Fifth," Maya told her. "Want to meet us?"

"Sure!" answered Joy. "We can meet at my place if you want. You're almost there."

Joy closed her phone and mostly ran the two blocks to her building. She wanted to be out of her dorky school uniform before Maya and Carolyn got there.

When the doorman announced that Carolyn and Maya were there, she was in black jeans and a fuzzy short-sleeved blue sweater. I should have picked up snack stuff on the way home, she thought. But then I wouldn't have had time to change.

The apartment doorbell rang. My *friends* are here, Joy thought as she opened the door to Maya and Carolyn. They must really like me to just drop by like this.

"Hi," Carolyn said cheerily. A big, toothy smile spread across her face. "How's it going?"

Joy and Maya exchanged a glance. They both could tell that Carolyn was trying to sound happy but really wasn't.

Joy found a big bottle of soda and some apples. Maya, remembering where the glasses were, took out three and filled them with ice. They sat at the kitchen table.

"What'd you lucky guys do with your afternoon off?" Joy asked.

"Spied on my father and his girlfriend," Carolyn blurted out.

Joy put down the apple that was halfway to her mouth. "You what?!"

"She wasn't spying," corrected Maya. She turned to Carolyn and added gently, "Tell her what happened."

Carolyn told Joy about the carriage ride and seeing her father and M. G. She tried to make her report sound funny — like a comic's monologue. Joy and Maya weren't laughing.

"Was she the woman he introduced us to at the party?" Joy asked, interrupting her. "The one in the gold silk outfit?"

"That's her," agreed Carolyn. "The source of all my problems." She opened her hand as she ticked off the problems. "*One,* he saw me see them, so *two* now he knows I know, which means *three* I'll have to meet her, and *four* she'll come to my apartment for dinner, and *five* she'll want to go shopping with me and act like she's my best friend . . . or . . . or . . ." Her count-off hand dropped and her smile crumbled. The joking was over. She burst into tears. ". . . or act like she's my mother."

Maya put an arm around her shoulder. "It must be so hard."

"I'm sorry," added Joy, not knowing what else to say or how to comfort Carolyn.

I have to stop crying, Carolyn told herself. I want to be brave like Mom wants me to be. She wiped her eyes and blew her nose into a paper napkin. "I'm okay. I just don't know what's going to happen when I get home. My dad probably thinks I was spying on him. That I cut school to *trail* him."

"You left a message on his answering machine that you didn't have school this afternoon," Maya reminded her. "He'll figure out that it was a coincidence that you were in the park when he listens to his messages."

"Then he'll punish me for taking a carriage ride without permission."

"Doesn't he know you're taking pictures of carriage horses?" asked Joy.

"Good point," agreed Maya.

Carolyn took a gulp of soda. She felt a little better. It was good to talk it all over with her friends. "I didn't tell him yet about my project. If I didn't even talk to him about *that,* how am I going to talk about this stuff?"

Maya stood up and paced the kitchen. "We need a plan."

"I think you should tell him that just because you know about him and Dr. Geng doesn't mean you want to hang out with her," suggested Joy. "That he shouldn't include you in their dates. And by the way, always call her *Doctor* Geng. It's a way of letting them know that you don't want to get too cozy with her. My first big mistake with Sue was calling her by her first name when she started dating my dad. From that moment on, she acted like we were best friends."

"I don't know how to explain any of this to my father," said Carolyn. "I'll get so nervous — and probably cry. I'll definitely mess it up."

Maya pointed a finger at her. "You will *not* mess it up. You just need to practice."

"Good idea," agreed Joy.

"Practice?" said Carolyn.

"We'll act out what you're going to say to your father," explained Maya. "I'll be him."

"Joy, will you be me, then?" asked Carolyn. "I want to hear how you'd tell him."

Joy smiled and tilted her head. "O-kay," she chirped in a cheery, high-pitched voice. "I'll be you."

Carolyn finally smiled again. "Very funny." She bopped Joy with her straw. "Be serious. This might actually help."

Joy stood up. "I'm you and I'm just coming home," she said in her regular Joy voice. "Your father is already there." She walked out of the kitchen and stood in the doorway.

Maya took a pair of Joy's mother's reading glasses and a newspaper from the counter. She sat at the table reading the paper with the eyeglasses perched halfway down her nose the way Carolyn's father wore his.

Joy came into the room. "Hi, Dad."

Maya-as-Dr. Kuhlberg looked over his glasses at her. "Hello, Carolyn." She glanced at the kitchen clock. "You're a few minutes late."

"Sorry, Dad," answered Joy-as-Carolyn.

Maya-as-Dr. Kuhlberg put the paper down and took off his glasses. "So you saw me in the park with Dr. Geng. I'm sure you realize that she is my lady friend. Maxine and I have been friends for a while now and I want you two to be friends, too."

Joy-as-Carolyn sat at the table. "I am sure Dr. Geng is very nice, Dad. But, I'd rather not become friends with her. I'd rather not hang out with you guys."

" 'Hang out', Carolyn?" said Maya-as-Dr. Kuhlberg.

"You know I don't like you using slang. Please be more precise in your speech."

"Yes, Dad," said Joy-as-Carolyn, her voice cracking with laughter.

Carolyn broke into laughter, too.

"Girls, girls," said Maya-as-Dr. Kuhlberg. "Try to have a little self-control."

Joy and Carolyn laughed even harder. So did Maya.

# Pizza Place

Carolyn ran up 81$^{st}$ Street. If she hurried, she could be home before her father. She saw Ivy George coming out of the building with two poodles and Precious.

Precious yapped a hello to Carolyn and Ivy looked up.

"Hey, Red," Ivy called.

Carolyn waved. When they met mid-block, Precious sniffed Carolyn's hand and she patted him.

"I just saw your dad," Ivy said. "He's in a great mood today."

"He is?"

"Yeah," answered Ivy. "He was whistling 'You Are My Sunshine.'"

"He was?"

Ivy looked at Carolyn quizzically. "He was even on pitch."

"Was he?"

Ivy stared at Carolyn. "Yeah. He was. He was on pitch. What's up with you today? You keep asking me if I mean what I say."

"I do?"

Ivy snapped her fingers. "There. You just did it again!"

Carolyn said, "Sorry." She *was* sorry. She liked Ivy and didn't want to annoy her. She wished she could tell her about the problems with her dad and M. G. But now she had to get home. "I have to go, Ivy," she said. "Or I'll be late."

With a wink, Ivy asked, "You will?" She signaled the dogs to move on. "Take care of yourself, Red. *You're* your dad's sunshine."

No, I'm not, thought Carolyn as she continued up the block. M. G. is my dad's sunshine.

When Carolyn came into the apartment, her father was sitting at the counter going through the mail. He looked at her over the top of his reading glasses — just the way Maya did when she play-acted him.

"Hi, honey," he said. "I got your message. What great weather to have the afternoon off. Today was the kind of day that makes you believe in spring, wasn't it?"

She nodded and thought, Why is he so cheerful? Doesn't he wonder why I was in a horse-drawn carriage? Isn't he embarrassed that I saw him holding hands with M. G.? She remembered the moment. The carriage was moving and there was a road between him and us. But I know he recognized me. He looked so surprised.

"Carolyn, there's something we have to talk about," he said solemnly.

Here it comes, thought Carolyn.

"I have been spending a great deal of time with Dr. Geng," he went on. "Dr. Geng — Maxine and I — have been dating. We met at a conference before I went to Thailand. She was on the trip, too."

Carolyn remembered Joy's parting advice: "Don't let him control the conversation. Be sure to get in what *you* want to say."

"I'm sure that Dr. Geng is a nice person, Dad. But she's your friend, not my friend. I don't want to hang out or go shopping with her or anything. Okay?" She bit her tongue. It sounded so lame. And she'd said *hang out* just like Joy did.

But for once he didn't correct her use of English. Instead he used his understanding-dad voice to say, "That's all right, Carolyn. Your response is normal and to be expected. But I need adult company. I enjoy the company of Dr. Geng."

"But Mom —"

He put up his hand to stop her from going on. "No one is going to try to replace your mother, Carolyn. No one can. For me, either." He sighed and looked down at his hands fan-folding a piece of junk mail. "Sometimes I think I see her. Then I have to accept that she's gone all over again." He looked at Carolyn and held her with his sad eyes. "Today — in the park — I saw a woman with your mother's wonderful red hair.

The sun was in my eyes so I couldn't see her clearly. She was in a horse-drawn carriage. And I had this feeling that it was her. I thought — for an instant — that we had her back." His eyes filled with tears. "Then, of course, I knew it wasn't her. Just someone with hair like hers."

Carolyn leaned toward him and said softly, "Dad, that was me. I was in the carriage. I saw you and Dr. Geng."

While they made dinner she told him all about Jolly and the carriage ride. Then she told him how she calmed Maximillian.

After dinner, she showed him Joy's photo of her and Maximillian. As they did the dishes, they told each other stories about her mother's special ability to communicate with horses. Carolyn knew all the stories her father told and he knew the ones she told. But they both loved hearing them again.

Later, when she said good night, he gave her a hug. "I'm proud of you for rescuing that runaway horse. You inherited more from your mother than just her red hair."

Shana didn't call Maya on Sunday or Monday or any other day that week. Maya thought she'd see her at Pizza Place after school on Friday. Since Maya went to a different school, it was a regular start-of-the-weekend meeting place for them. Delores and Jay-Cee were already there. But Shana was a no-show.

"She said she had something else to do,"

Delores explained. She rolled her eyes. "With Alex, for sure. Uh-huh. They are together now."

"Maybe she's not here because she's mad at me," Maya thought out loud.

Delores wasn't listening. She turned toward the noise of four tough girls coming into Pizza Place. Maya looked over. It was Loreen and three other girls who went to the same school as Shana, Jay-Cee, and Delores.

"Yo, D-Girl," one of them called to Delores.

"Yo," Delores yelled back.

Jay-Cee counted out her change for a slice. "Shana's not mad at you, M," she said. "She's in *luv*."

I wish, thought Maya.

The three friends took their slices and sodas to a booth. While they ate, Jay-Cee drew a new design for a halter top on the back of a place mat.

They were clearing out of the booth when Maya brought up the arts festival at the Apollo. "I thought Shana might do it. You know perform that poem she did at the slam. Or another one. I left the flyer for it at her place."

"There were notices about that at school," said Delores. "I told her she should do it. But she said no."

"Why?" asked Jay-Cee.

"Didn't say why," answered Delores.

I know why, thought Maya. She's not doing it because I'm in it. And she thinks if I am, Carolyn and Joy are, too.

"Too bad she's not," commented Jay-Cee.

Maya dropped her paper cup and oil-stained paper plate into the trash. "Yeah, it is too bad."

After school on Monday, Joy went right home. She was — as usual — alone in the apartment. But this time, her mother wasn't at her office. Today she was working on a Caribbean island. St. Barts. She was going to be gone for a whole week and Joy was going to her dad's.

She changed out of her uniform into her black jeans and a black velvet top, patted her face with an almost white powder, and applied black lipstick. It was so quiet in the apartment. So empty. She put on the Big Bang Band CD and danced to Ivy's percussive sound. It was fun to feel good about going to her dad's. Fun to look forward to seeing Jake. She didn't particularly look forward to living with Sue for a week. But the important thing was that she felt closer to her dad — more like she was the "Joy of his life," like she used to be before Jake was born. She remembered how he criticized her Goth look. He'll get used to it, she decided.

Joy stopped dancing and started packing.

The first thing that surprised her when she got to her dad's was that he was there. Her workaholic dad home in the afternoon? The second surprise was that he was lying on the couch, channel-surfing. On a weekday. He barely said hello.

"Are you sick, Dad?"

"No," he answered as he surfed from a game show to CNN.

She put down her suitcase. "Did you take the day off?"

"Sort of." CNN became Court TV. "Needed a break."

He finally got up to greet her. "Haven't you gotten over dressing like death yet?" he asked. "I'd kiss you, but I'm afraid whatever you've got is catching."

He laughed at his own joke.

She didn't.

Sue came into the room with Jake in her arms. "Just up from his nap," Sue explained as she handed him over to Joy. His body slumped against her and he murmured, "Oy." She kissed his sleep-sweaty head.

Her father was back on the couch, remote in hand. What's going on? Joy wondered. He hates TV. He's always saying it's a colossal waste of time — unless it's business news.

"Aren't you coming with Jake and me for a walk, Ted?" Sue asked. "It stopped raining. We have to pick up something for dinner."

"Can't you see I'm busy?" he snapped. "I have to keep in touch with what's going on."

"Right. Okay," Sue snapped back at him. She looked over at Joy. "I'm taking Jake out. Do you want to come?"

"I have homework," Joy said, handing Jake back.

"I like your top," Sue commented. "It's flattering."

"Don't encourage her," Joy's father barked.

Joy went to her room and closed the door.

At half past twelve on Saturday, Carolyn met Maya in the third subway car from the front of the downtown number 9. Maya made room for Carolyn to sit next to her. They read Maya's *Daily News* the rest of the way downtown.

As Carolyn stepped out of the car at the Eighth Street stop, she spotted a tall boy with growing-out bleached hair on the platform. "It's Serge!" she exclaimed.

Maya followed her off the train. "Where?"

Carolyn pointed. "By that big trash bin. Where we used to leave him newspapers. Look. He's putting one down."

As Maya saw Serge, he saw her. He pointed to the paper he'd just placed on the edge of the bin, grinned, and disappeared into the crowd going up the stairs.

Carolyn and Maya moved toward the trash can. An elderly gentleman in a business suit picked up Serge's paper before they got to it.

Carolyn nudged Maya and whispered, "Say something."

"Excuse me, sir," Maya began. "Uh — that's — uh — sort of my paper."

The man looked at her, confused. "I beg your pardon, miss. I just saw a young man leave it." He pointed to the newspaper in Maya's hand. "Besides, you have your own newspaper."

Maya held out her copy of the *Daily News*. "I'll change papers with you," she said. "They're the same, except our friend left us a note in that one."

"I don't have time for this," said the man above the rumble of a train pulling into the station.

"But we need *that* paper," pleaded Carolyn.

"I didn't think young people read the paper anymore," the man grumbled as he handed Maya the paper. He took hers and rushed toward the opening doors of the train.

Carolyn grabbed Maya's arm and pulled her toward a bench in the middle of the platform. "Hurry up. Open it," she directed as they sat down.

In the centerfold were photos of people battling the storm that hit the city the day before. Gutters overflowing. A passing cab splashing a pedestrian. Sleet and wind pushing a woman down the street, her umbrella inside-out. Serge had printed his message in red ink across the stormy-day pictures. It was written like a poem. It was a poem. Sort of.

> HI YA, MAYA.
> I WANT TO KNOW ENGLISH WELL
> SO NO ONE I MEET CAN TELL
> I AM NEW TO U S OF A
> LIKE GUY WHO CAME FROM RUSSIA YESTERDAY.
> SERGE.

P.S. CAN I GO TO ARTS FESTIVAL AT APOLLO
WITH YOU, CAROLYN, AND JOY? ALEX IS GO-
ING WITH SHANA ON DATE.

Carolyn read Serge's rhyme again and smiled.
"That is so cute."

"It is," agreed Maya.

Carolyn stood up. "I'm glad he's going with us.
That's good news."

Maya closed the paper and thought, For me it's
good news–bad news. Good news: Serge is going to
the festival with us. Bad news: Shana will be there
and see me with even more white friends.

When Maya and Carolyn got to class, Joy was already there. Maya handed her the newspaper. She
didn't have to tell Joy there was a message from
Serge. Joy could see it in Carolyn's grin.

Joy opened the paper. By the time she finished
the message, she was grinning, too.

Charlie sat next to Carolyn.

"Are you going to try out for that arts festival,
Charlie?" Carolyn asked him.

He nodded. "But I don't think I'm going to the
show. It's way uptown, and I live in Brooklyn."

"It's not so far on the subway. And you can meet
up with us," Carolyn offered. The instant it was out of
her mouth, she thought, I should have checked with
Maya and Joy before inviting him.

"Thanks," Charlie said. "That'd be great."

Carolyn looked at Maya to see if it was okay that she'd invited him. Maya shrugged. She was imagining Charlie, with his limited vision, arriving at the crowded theater and trying to find them. She'd have to really watch out for him. One more person she'd have to chaperone.

Beth strode into the room. "Let's go, gang. First, we'll talk about what you're printing today. Next, I'll teach you more about blocking. Then it's off to the darkroom. By the time you leave today, I need prints for the Shout It/Show It Arts Festival. How many of you are giving me prints?"

Joy raised her hand and looked around the room. Janice, Charlie, Maya, and Carolyn were the only ones with hands raised. "Only half of you?" Beth asked. "Do you think I should be satisfied with that? Huh? The answer is no. I don't think so! I want *everyone* represented. You don't have to go to the festival, but I want your prints there."

By the time the session was over, Beth had a print from each of the workshop participants. And Joy had an idea of a note for Serge. She even had a copy of the *Village Voice* in her backpack that they could use. On the way out of the workshop, she told her idea to Maya and Carolyn.

"I love it," said Carolyn.

Maya took a blue marker out of her bag. "Let's do it."

They stopped in the lobby and opened the

paper. Maya printed the message across the center-fold.

DEAR NEW AMERICAN POET:
FOR PHOTOS AND TO LISTEN TO POETRY
MEET US AT REMEMBER ME
BE THERE AT SEVEN O'CLOCK
AND WE WILL WALK DOWN THE BLOCK
TO THE APOLLO THEATER.
MAYA WILL BE OUR LEADER.
MAYA, CAROLYN, AND JOY.

"We'll tell Charlie to meet us at the store, too," said Maya.

Joy closed the paper. "Let's go drop this off at Serge's building," Joy suggested. "Maybe stop for a soda or something on the way."

"I have to go uptown right away," Maya announced. "I promised my mom I'd pick up Hannah and Naomi at a birthday party."

Joy turned to Carolyn. "Can you?"

Carolyn checked her watch. "I told Dad I'd be home early tonight."

"I guess that makes you Solo Messenger Girl," said Maya.

"I guess," agreed Joy, already missing them.

Maya and Carolyn headed west to the train.

As Joy walked east, she remembered that Serge worked Saturday afternoons at Zeus — a tattoo and piercing parlor. I could bring him the paper there, she thought. But if I go to Zeus, I might see Wren.

Wren who worked at Zeus.

Wren who crashed my party.

Wren who tried to steal my ring.

I'll write Serge's name on the front of the paper and leave it with his uncle.

After Joy left the paper for Serge, she went to her dad's. She had to pack her things and go uptown to her mother's. I want to leave Dad's before dinner, she decided. I don't want to eat with him and Sue. He's been in such a lousy mood all week. He and Sue are so stressed out.

Sue was in Joy's bedroom on the treadmill, fast-walking to nowhere. "Thanks for letting me put this in here," she told Joy.

"Where's Dad?" Joy asked.

"He took Jake to the park so I could exercise in peace."

"I have to pack," Joy announced.

"Go ahead," Sue huffed. "You won't be in my way."

Maybe you're in *my* way, Joy thought as she pulled her suitcase out of the closet.

She packed. Sue walked. The only sound in the room was her aerobic breathing.

Finally, Sue broke the silence. "Your father doesn't want you to know, but I'm sure you've guessed by now."

A moment of panic shot through Joy. Were Sue and her father getting divorced? She didn't like Sue that much, but she didn't want Jake to have divorced parents like her. He was just a baby.

"Guessed what?" Joy asked.

Sue adjusted the slant of the board to walk uphill. "That your father lost his job. He was fired."

Relief replaced panic. They weren't getting a divorce. Jake was safe. For now. "How come he didn't tell me?" she asked.

"He was hoping he'd get another job . . . and could tell you he lost one . . . and he has a new one . . . at the same time." Sue was running out of breath. "He's been . . . out of work . . . for a month now."

"Maybe you should slow that thing down," Joy suggested.

"It's okay. . . . I eat when I'm upset. . . . Gained a pound last week. . . . Got to take it off."

"Whatever," said Joy. "If he doesn't go to work, where does he go every day? He left with me last week when I went to school. He had on a suit."

"The company gave him a little office with a computer and a telephone. . . . All the stuff he needs to look for another job. . . . But there are no other jobs. . . . People are being laid off all over Wall Street. . . . One-third of the people in his office were fired."

Joy folded a sweater and put it in the suitcase. "Dad will get another job," she said. "My dad's a workaholic."

Sue started the slow-down phase of her workout. "I never thought this would happen to us." Tears rolled into the sweat on her cheeks.

"He's always made lots of money," Joy said. "Really. Don't worry."

"I'll try not to." Sue looked at the odometer on her exercise machine. "That burned up two hundred calories. Every little bit helps." She stepped off the treadmill and put a hand on Joy's shoulder. "Thanks."

For what? Joy thought as Sue finally left the room. For letting you put your stupid exercise machine in my room? Or for telling you my dad would always have lots of money?

"Close the door, please," she called after Sue.

But she was already gone. In the kitchen, thought Joy, deciding what to eat that's only two hundred calories.

She closed the door herself.

# West Broadway

For the arts festival, Maya dressed in black cargo pants, hiking boots, gray T-shirt, and denim jacket. Her nine-year-old sister, Hannah, had put a dozen braids in her hair and pulled them back into a ponytail.

Maya checked herself in the mirror and liked what she saw. Simple. Nothing to call attention to herself. She wished she'd told Joy and Carolyn to dress down, too. If Carolyn wore one of her little-girl outfits and Joy went full Goth, they'd stick out more than ever in the neighborhood crowd. She glanced at her clock radio. It was too late to call them. They'd be on their way by now.

Hannah was carefully arranging her hairdressing tools in a shoe box. The top of the box was covered with a collage of hairdos cut from glossy magazines and read: PROPERTY OF HANNAH JOHNSON. HAIRSTYLIST.

Maya picked up a pair of jeans from the floor. "Joy and Carolyn are coming for a sleepover tonight, Hannah. Help me clean up my room. Okay?"

"I can't. I'm busy. I have an appointment to braid Naomi's hair next. I have to get ready." She put the top on the box. "I have responsibilities, Maya."

"Which you take a little too seriously," complained Maya. "*Please* help me make this bed."

Hannah carefully placed her box on the bureau and stood beside the bed to help make it. "Do you think Carolyn will let me braid her hair?"

Maya grinned at the thought of Carolyn's straight red hair in cornrows. "I bet she would."

Carolyn wrinkled her nose at her mirrored self. Freckles. Ugh. She brushed dusty-green eye shadow on her lids. She was wearing an A-line denim skirt and the green sweater set she'd bought at Remember Me. She opened her jewelry box and took out the little dangling horse earrings her mother had given her. Joy doesn't like these, she thought. Well, I don't like some of her earrings — especially the skulls. As she put in the earrings she thought, Maybe other people won't like my earrings, either. Like Shana. She flipped her hair over the little gold horses. Will Shana be there tonight? she wondered. If she is, I'll be extra nice to her. For Maya's sake.

The intercom buzzer rang from downstairs.

"I'll get it," her father shouted from the other room.

Joy told me she's wearing a Goth outfit tonight, Carolyn remembered. But I don't want to have to deal with Dad's reaction to that. "Tell Joy to wait for me downstairs," she called to her father. She grabbed her sleepover bag from the bed and left her room.

"You look lovely," her father said when she came into the living room. "Don't forget to be home by noon tomorrow. We have a one o'clock brunch date with the Felders. They're looking forward to seeing you."

Carolyn was looking forward to seeing the Felders, too. They were family friends who owned the ranch next to her grandparents. "I won't forget," she agreed — already trying to figure out if she could eat Maya's Sunday morning pancakes *and* brunch in a restaurant.

She opened the door to leave.

"Since you're at Maya's tonight," he added. "I might stay late at Dr. Geng's. I'll have my cell phone if you need me."

"Okay, Dad." At least Dr. Geng isn't staying here, she thought as she closed the door behind her.

When Maya came into her mother's store, Charlie, Joy, and Carolyn were already there. Her hope of being inconspicuous at the Apollo slipped away when she saw them.

Joy had on her most dramatic Goth outfit — long lacy black skirt, pointy boots, tight velvet top with wide, flowing sleeves, skull earrings, and almost-black lipstick.

Carolyn was dressed like the sweet girl she was — pretty and preppy.

Charlie, at least, was dressed down in jeans and a loose football shirt with a number 39 on it.

"Your mom said she'd take our overnight bags to your house," Joy announced.

"Where's Jay-Cee?" Maya asked, looking around for the one black friend going with her.

Before anyone could answer, Jay-Cee came out of the dressing room. She was in one of her Jay-Cee original animal-print skirts, boots, and a deep-orange sweater.

Maya looked around at the mismatched group. "Well," she said. "Let's go."

"But Serge isn't here, yet," Joy reminded her.

"Or Delores," added Carolyn.

"Delores is meeting us there," Maya told them.

"And Serge is here," announced Carolyn, pointing to the door.

Serge walked in, grinning. His hair was freshly bleached and streaked with green instead of the usual purple. "Sorry I am late — for our date."

Joy returned his grin and asked, "Are you going to rhyme — all the time?"

"I am making my English teacher crazy," he answered. "But she is happy I am not lazy."

Carolyn and Jay-Cee joined Joy in a collective groan.

"Maybe you should stop rhyming for a while," advised Joy.

"Shakespeare makes rhyme, too," he countered.

"Not quite the same," laughed Joy.

"Shakespeare's weren't lame," added Charlie.

More groans.

With a sweeping motion, Serge told the girls they

should go out the door ahead of him. Joy thought, he's cute, he's funny, and he's a gentleman.

Maya thought, he's really acting silly tonight. I hope he calms down before we get to the Apollo.

The crowd outside the theater and in the lobby was young, noisy, hip, and mostly black. Maya led her group through the crowd into the theater.

Some guy Maya knew from her block said, "Hey, Maya," as she passed. She imagined him thinking, "What's Maya Johnson doing with all those white kids?"

Joy spotted a pile of programs on a chair at the entrance to the hall. She picked up six and handed them around to their group.

Carolyn took one and checked out the hall. The crowd, she noticed, was a real mix. There were Asian kids, Latinos, a little of everything. But no other redheads that she could see. She didn't feel as odd about being white as she did at the poetry slam. The walls of the big space, she could see, were covered with photographs. One of those is mine, she thought proudly. She checked out the stage. A DJ was spinning music in front of a huge photograph of a Harlem street scene. She nudged Maya and pointed to the stage. "That photo looks like one of yours."

Maya recognized the shot. But it wasn't hers. "That's a Gordon Parks photo," she said. "He's a famous photographer."

"I never heard of him," admitted Carolyn.

"Well, he's famous all over," snapped Maya. "Not just in Harlem."

Carolyn, confused and hurt, looked down at her program.

I was just mean to her, thought Maya. But, really, don't white people know who Gordon Parks is? I know the names of a lot of *white* photographers.

"We're in the program," Carolyn said to anyone who was interested. She flipped the page. The names of poets were listed, too. "Shana's here."

Maya checked out the poets' page in her own program and saw Shana's name. She turned to Jay-Cee. "I thought she wasn't going to be in it."

Jay-Cee shrugged her shoulders. "That's what she said. I guess she changed her mind."

Charlie looked around the hall and asked, "Where are our photos?"

"They're hung all around," answered Carolyn. "On the walls."

Charlie can't see the pictures from here, thought Maya. Even with his thick glasses. Can he tell how dark a person's skin is? Or does everyone's skin look the same to him?

Joy turned herself in a slow circle to check out the exhibit. The first picture she recognized was a big print Charlie had made of his sister's face.

"I see your picture," she told Charlie. "It looks good, even from here."

"All our pictures must be in that section," commented Carolyn. "Beth said they'd be hung together."

"Let's go look," Serge said, ready to lead the

way. "You are all famous people tonight. I am with the very best people for being here."

I'm *not* with the best people for being here, thought Maya. She spotted Shana and Alex coming into the hall. She didn't want Shana to see her with Carolyn and Maya. "You guys go ahead," she said quickly. "I have to check something out."

"I'll stay with you," Carolyn offered.

"No!" Maya said with an edge of impatience. "I'll catch you later, okay?"

"Okay," agreed Carolyn. Maya walked away and left her there.

Why is she being so grumpy? Carolyn wondered. She's acting like she wishes I weren't here.

A voice hissed in Carolyn's ear, "Are you one of Maya's new friends?" She looked over her shoulder. A girl glared at her. Fear rippled through Carolyn. She spotted Serge's blond-and-green head and rushed to catch up with him.

Maya waved to Alex and Shana. Alex waved back before jumping up on the stage and heading toward the DJ. Shana walked toward Maya. The two friends met in front of the stage.

"Hey," said Maya in their familiar way.

Shana sort of smiled. "Hey back. So you got pictures hanging here."

"Just one." She added, "The whole workshop had to do it," so Shana would know that it wasn't her fault that Carolyn and Joy were in the show. Or that they were at the arts festival.

"You doing the same poem you did the other night?" Maya asked.

"Girl, I'm not doing no poem," Shana shot back.

"You're on the program," said Maya.

"Not," said Shana.

Maya opened her program and pointed to Shana's name. "It says here."

Shana saw her name and angrily slapped the page. "I — did — not — sign — up."

Maya closed the program. "Well you should have. Your poetry is good. It's real. It happened to you."

"That's why I *don't* want to do it!" protested Shana. "At the slam I felt like I was on some dumb tell-all talk show."

"It was poetry," said Maya. "I'm really sorry I didn't know when all that happened. Like that time your arm was all black and blue and you came over to my house to make pancakes." She heard herself rattling on, but now that she was finally talking to Shana she couldn't stop herself. "Besides, it helps other people to hear that stuff about you and your mother. I left you that notice about tonight with a note saying we should talk. That's what I want us to —"

The anger flashing in Shana's eyes stopped Maya mid-sentence.

"You signed me up for this. *You* did it. Now I gotta be a no-show. Means I gotta leave now. Girl, you have crossed a line."

"I didn't sign you up, Shana," Maya protested. "Why would I do that?"

"Because you're a busybody thinking you're some kinda psychic. Because you think you know what's good for everyone." Shana jabbed her finger in Maya's direction. "Well — you — don't."

"Hey, Alex," a cheerful voice called. Maya saw Charlie, Carolyn, Joy, Jay-Cee, and Serge join up with Alex. They were all headed toward Shana and Maya.

"Your *friends* are here," Shana said to Maya under her breath.

"That DJ is cool," Alex announced when he reached them. "I'm going to dance while he spins." He popped and locked his arms as if to prove the point.

"And Shana's doing poetry," said Carolyn with a smile in her direction. "I'm so glad you changed your mind."

Maya shot Carolyn a glance that said, Please don't say that, but it was too late.

"I did not and I am not," said Shana. "It was Maya's idea." She glared at Maya again. "And a lousy one."

Alex threw an arm around Shana's shoulder. "I'm the one signed you up."

Shana pulled away from him. "You did that?!" She frowned. "Without telling me?"

"If I'd told you, you'd've said no," explained Alex. "Here's what I think. You should perform your new poem hip-hop, the way we did the other night. I'll do my break dance. I talked to the DJ about it. Gave him the records."

Shana was still frowning, still deciding — Joy thought — whether to be angry at Alex or not.

Alex brushed Shana's cheek with the back of his hand. "I thought if we did it together, it'd be all right. Come on. Say you're glad."

"I guess it's okay," agreed Shana.

"That's so sweet," Carolyn cooed. She covered her mouth with her hand the moment the word "sweet" came out.

Shana shot her a scowl. "What did you say?"

"She said, 'That's so 'beat',' " Joy answered for Carolyn. "It means it's cool. It's a compliment."

"It's something her grandfather is always saying," added Maya, suddenly feeling protective of Carolyn.

Shana's scowl moved to Joy. "Sounds like her grandfather got it wrong," she said.

"Sor-ry," muttered Joy.

Alex gave Shana's arm a little tug. "We gotta go work this thing out with the DJ." He grinned at the others. "Catch you all later."

Shana hated me when she thought I signed her up to perform, thought Maya. But when she found out Alex did it, it was okay. What's that all about?

Serge tapped Maya on the shoulder. "Your photo looks excellent, Maya. Come see."

"Okay," she agreed. "Might as well."

Maya was walking across the hall with her friends when she spotted Delores with Loreen and

**107**

her crew. Maya thought Delores would come over and say something like, "I was looking all over for you guys." Instead, she made a one-hundred-and-eighty-degree turn. To avoid us, thought Maya. One of Loreen's friends — a tall girl with short hair in cornrows — noticed Maya and said something to the girl next to her. That girl looked at Maya and sneered. A chill ran up Maya's arms.

"There's Delores," Carolyn told Maya. Her face lit up and she went over to her. "We were looking for you."

Delores nodded a small hello.

Carolyn recognized the girl standing next to Delores. She was the one who'd asked what she was doing there. Well, now she knows that I'm friends with Maya and Delores, thought Carolyn. So it's going to be okay. "Hi," Carolyn said to the girl. "I'm Carolyn."

"Yeah?" said the girl as she flashed a mean-edged grin. "It's an *honor* to meet you, Car-o-lyn."

Carolyn willed herself to ignore the sarcastic tone and unkind vibe. *Concentrate on the positive,* her grandfather would say. She turned to Delores, "Did you see Maya's photograph? It's just like something Gordon Parks would do."

The shortest of the four girls took Carolyn, Joy, Charlie, and Serge in with a sweeping look. "You all took pictures for this?"

"I did not take pictures," admitted Serge.

"But the rest of us did," said Charlie proudly.

Maya heard the third girl mumble to Delores, "Even four-eyes, huh?"

"Let's go look at those photos," directed Loreen.

A queasy feeling seeped through Maya, a feeling she often felt around Loreen.

*They're only pretending to be interested.*

*They're just doing it to make fun of us.*

# Apollo Theater

The music stopped suddenly and a voice shouted through the loudspeaker, "Welcome the man — your MC, Rafiq!"

Heads turned toward the stage. Rafiq — dreadlocks flying — ran out to center stage. Perfect timing, thought Maya. *We won't be looking at our photos with Loreen.*

While the crowd clapped and cheered, Maya steered her group away from Loreen and her friends. She motioned for Delores to come, too. But Delores wouldn't look at her.

Maya remembered when Delores always hung out with her, Shana, and Jay-Cee. Her dad used to call them the Mighty Four. *Now Delores is in with girls we used to avoid. Is it my fault because I'm hanging out so much with my friends from the photography workshop?*

Rafiq welcomed everyone, thanked the organizers of the festival, and congratulated the photographers on their exhibit. "Now," he announced, "it's time to give it up for the poets."

"Who's judging?" someone shouted.

"We're not scoring tonight," answered Rafiq. "We're showcasing. So *show* what you think of the poems by clapping."

"Or booing," another voice called out.

A few practice boos came from around the hall.

"I hope Shana's first," Carolyn told Jay-Cee.

"She won't be," Jay-Cee explained. "She's using music and has a dancer. She'll be in the hip-hop section."

The first poet's poem was about how his parents expected him to be the top student in his class and how it was messing up his life.

The audience mostly liked it. There were only a few boos at the end.

There were nine more poems. Carolyn laughed at some and was close to tears during others.

Joy thought the performances were first-rate. A few of the poems were like Shana's poem from the slam — honest about painful things going on in the poet's life.

Maya liked the group poems best. Three poets performed one protesting war. Another group performed a hilarious poem about all the different foods you could find in New York City, including broccoli ice cream and chocolate-covered ants.

Joy looked around at the crowd of laughing and clapping kids. She made eye contact with a stranger and they exchanged smiles. This is a great event, Joy thought. With my photo on exhibit, I'm really part of it.

Shana and Alex were the last hip-hop act.

The DJ spun their records. Shana slapped her thigh and performed her poem/song in a rapid fire of words. The lyrics were about being strong and independent and not letting other people tell you what to do. Alex punctuated the poem with his movements. Their performance was short but perfect. The audience went wild.

Rafiq's voice sliced through the applause. "We'll be seeing more of *that* sister."

Carolyn thought Shana's hip-hop number was terrific. She admired her. But she still didn't like her. How can I like her, she thought, when she doesn't like me? Why would I?

Even though it felt like they weren't best friends anymore, Maya was proud of Shana and happy for her. She was still clapping when a voice behind her said, "Why are you bringing all these new people up here? Your *old* friends not good enough for you?"

Maya turned around to see who said it. She faced a group of guys. It wasn't them. The voice was female.

*Did Joy and Carolyn hear?*

Maya turned to her right. Joy was smiling and clapping still. She hadn't heard. She turned to her left. Carolyn's face registered wide-eyed alarm. She had heard.

"Did you see who was behind me?" Maya shouted to Carolyn.

Carolyn nodded. "Delores's friend. That tall girl. Loreen."

*Loreen.* Chills ran along Maya's arms. *She's always had it in for me.*

"You got six seconds to report to the dance floor!" Rafiq announced.

The DJ took over and everyone on the floor began moving.

While Serge danced with Carolyn and Joy, Maya looked for Jay-Cee.

*I have to tell her about Loreen.*

Maya was inching through the crowd toward Jay-Cee when someone grabbed her hand from behind and pulled.

*Loreen. What is she going to do?*

The hand pulled Maya around. But it wasn't Loreen or anyone from her gang. It was Serge, dancing in front of her, wanting her to dance with him.

*Serge was dancing with Carolyn and Joy a minute ago. Where are they now?*

She leaned toward him. "Where are Carolyn and Joy?"

"They went to the room for the girls," he answered.

She stopped dancing and quickly scanned the hall. *The way Loreen's acting, I should go with them.* She spotted a flash of red hair. Carolyn.

"I'll be right back," she told Serge.

As Carolyn followed Joy to the restroom, she noticed Loreen going in the same direction. "Let's go back," she started to tell Joy.

But Joy didn't hear her. She had found the restroom and was pushing the door open.

Carolyn followed her in.

Joy went into a stall before Carolyn could tell her about Loreen.

While Carolyn waited for her, she checked out her own reflection in the mirror.

Three other faces appeared with hers. Loreen was behind Carolyn. Two of her girlfriends stood at the sink on either side of her.

"Where's Maya?" Loreen asked.

A spray of water splashed Carolyn's arm.

"Oops. Sor-ry," said the girl to her right.

Carolyn brushed the water off her arm. Did she do that on purpose? she wondered. The look on the girl's face answered the question.

"I asked you — where's Maya?" Loreen repeated. She glanced toward the stalls. "Is she hiding? Scared?"

"Maya's not in here," Carolyn admitted. She wished she could keep the fear out of her voice.

Joy came out of the stall. Loreen looked her up and down. Joy could feel the tension in the air.

"Are *you* scared?" Loreen asked Joy.

"No," Joy lied. "Why should I be?"

Carolyn touched Joy's arm and indicated the door with a look that said, Let's get out of here.

Carolyn's heart was thumping as she walked out with Joy.

Maya had almost reached the restroom when

she saw Carolyn and Joy come out and slip into the crowd. She thought that they looked scared. Then she saw Loreen and two of her crew follow Carolyn and Joy out of the restroom.

Maya worked her way toward Carolyn and Joy. *Loreen is always making trouble, ever since we were little kids. Now she's bullying Carolyn and Joy to get to me. It's just like Loreen to do that.*

Maya caught up with her friends.

"Loreen's looking for you," Carolyn told Maya.

Maya took her hand. "Come on. We'll get lost in the crowd."

But it was too late. Loreen came around in front of Maya and blocked the way.

"Maya," Loreen said in a fake friendly voice, "I bumped into your downtown friends in the restroom. It doesn't look to me like they're having much fun. I think they want to go home." She smiled at Carolyn and Joy. "Don't you?"

Carolyn looked to Maya for an answer.

"No they don't," Maya told Loreen.

Loreen put her hands on her hips. "Well, I say they do. And I say you want to go, too."

Maya looked her straight in the eye. "We're supposed to be here. We have photos in the show. Remember? All you're showing, Loreen, is a lot of bad attitude. Get over it."

"You get over it," Loreen hissed. "Maya, you been bugging me for so long, I wake up in the morning mad. I'm sick of you and your cop daddy and your fancy brownstone. I'm sick of you all the time thinking you're so much better than everyone else."

"Well, I'm sick of your bullying," Maya shot back. "Now move."

"I don't think so," Loreen said as she stepped in closer to Maya.

Carolyn noticed that some kids had stopped dancing and were watching them. She exchanged a glance with Joy. What could they do?

Panic shot through Joy. Is this going to be a fight? she wondered. I don't know how to fight, but I will if I have to help Maya. She glared at Loreen. "Just leave us alone."

Loreen raised her eyebrows. "Us? As far as I'm concerned, you're already gone."

"Stop it, Loreen," warned Maya.

"What are you going to do?" Loreen hissed. "Call your daddy?"

Just then, Shana came out of the crowd and stood beside Maya. "Hey, Loreen," she said evenly. "What's up?"

Loreen switched her attention from Maya to Shana. "Nothing's up, and if it were, it wouldn't be any of your business."

Carolyn's heart pounded. Loreen was a head higher than Shana and a lot bigger.

Shana took another step closer to Loreen, looked up at her defiantly, then eased into a smile. "You don't want trouble, Loreen. You're too smart for that."

Delores was there, too, with Loreen. She jerked her head toward a security guard looking in their direction, and said, "Let's go."

Loreen gave Shana a long, hard stare. Then she turned away and disappeared with her friends into the crowd. Delores went with them.

The kids who'd been watching went back to dancing.

Alex came over and put a hand on Shana's shoulder. "Everything okay?"

"Everything's okay," agreed Shana.

"It is," agreed Maya. "Everything is okay."

Shana and Alex started dancing. Serge came over to Maya. As she danced with him, Maya had a flashback.

*Third grade. In the playground at recess. Loreen and her friends bullying me. Shana standing up for me. We become best friends instantly.*

Alex and Shana were dancing beside her and Serge now. Shana looked happy.

*I hope things are better with her mother. I hope she'll talk to me about it someday.* The familiar feeling of being Shana's best friend came back to her.

Maya touched Shana's arm. A smiling face turned to her. "Yeah? What?"

"Thanks," Maya said above the music. "Thanks for helping out with Loreen. Again."

"I never liked her," Shana said.

"She's trouble," agreed Maya.

Shana leaned closer. "Well the trouble's gone."

She flashed Maya a grin, turned, and danced away.

As Carolyn danced, she kept an eye out for Loreen, but she didn't see her. She remembered a fight at the ranch a few years before. Three of the ranch hands had gotten into an argument over something. She never knew what. One of the men punched her grandfather in the face when he tried to break it up. Her grandfather hadn't hit the guy back. A new thought pushed away the memory of Grandfather's broken nose. Was Loreen waiting outside for Maya?

Maya was thinking the same thing.

So was Joy.

At 9:30, Maya said it was time to leave. She'd promised her mother they'd be home by ten.

A few minutes later they were on the street. Loreen and her pals were nowhere in sight.

Serge and Charlie left to take the downtown train.

Jay-Cee lived a block from the Apollo. She said good night and headed home.

As Maya, Carolyn, and Joy walked down the street, Maya spotted Loreen and her group coming out of Pizza Place. They turned and walked the other way.

A bus was coming down the street. "Let's catch it," Maya said.

They ran across the street and met the bus just as it pulled up to the stop.

Maya didn't really relax until she walked into her own house and closed the door.

Her parents were on the couch in the living room watching a movie and eating popcorn.

Joy saw the popcorn and thought, I'm hungry.

"You girls have a good time?" Mrs. Johnson asked.

"Great," said Carolyn enthusiastically.

"There were a lot of people there," added Joy.

"It was really great," said Maya.

Her mother paused the video.

"What about your photographs?" her father asked. "How'd the show look?"

"Okay," answered Maya.

The three girls looked at one another and burst out laughing. So much had happened at the arts festival, they'd all forgotten that their photos were on exhibit.

"What's so funny?" asked Mr. Johnson.

"I guess it's an inside joke," answered his wife. She unpaused the video.

Carolyn took a deep breath to collect herself and said, "Sorry."

Joy said, "Enjoy the movie."

They followed Maya out of the room.

"I put your backpacks in Maya's room," Mrs. Johnson called after them.

The three friends stopped in the kitchen for

snacks to bring up to Maya's room. Carolyn was in charge of cookies and pretzels. Joy carried sodas. Maya found some grapes, apples, and a bag of chocolate kisses.

"No chocolate-covered ants?" teased Joy.

When they got to the room, they changed into their boxer shorts and T-shirts before sitting on the rug with their snacks.

Maya was thinking, What should I say about what happened tonight? when Carolyn said, "Don't worry about what happened tonight, Maya. Stuff like that goes on all the time. Not just in your neighborhood."

Maya stuck a straw in her soda can. "It wasn't about you being there. You know that, don't you?"

"Loreen was after *you*," said Joy. "That was clear."

"She's always looking for an excuse to bully me," explained Maya. "It's been that way forever. I just wish she'd get over it. Or move."

"Some people are just looking for an excuse to be mean," Joy added thoughtfully. "At my school, this girl Alicia decided that this other girl didn't look pretty enough to be in her group of friends."

"*Pretty* enough?" asked Carolyn, surprised. "That's dumb."

Joy raised her right hand. "I swear. Here's the weirdest part. The girl she was dissing was really pretty."

"And who decides what's pretty, anyway?" asked Maya. "Does 'pretty' mean looking like everybody else?"

"Take noses for example," put in Joy. "That's what Alicia said about this girl. I remember her name now. It was Caroline." She smiled at Carolyn. "But spelled the other way. With an *i* instead of a *y*. Anyway, Alicia went around saying that Caroline was ugly because she had a big nose."

Carolyn stroked her own nose. It was wide, like her mother's and grandfather's. Sometimes when she looked in the mirror, she pinched her nostrils to see how she'd look with a smaller nose. "My nose is pretty big," she said. "I guess I can't be Alicia's friend."

"Ah, poor you," teased Joy. "What a loss."

"I like big noses," said Maya. "I'm thinking of having mine enlarged."

"You are?" said Carolyn.

Joy tossed a pillow in Carolyn's direction. "You're so gullible, CK."

Maya threw a pillow at her, too. "That's what we love about you."

The next morning they made pancakes.

Naomi sat at the counter and watched Joy stirring the batter before pouring it onto the hot skillet.

"I want mine to be dinosaurs," Hannah said.

Joy looked over at her, surprised. "Dinosaur pancakes?"

Naomi nodded.

"I don't know how."

"Shana can do dinosaurs easy," Naomi reported. "And she makes Barney for Piper. But anybody can do hearts. So just make hearts for us."

"I'll try," agreed Joy, not sure she could do that, either.

Maya came up behind her sister and pulled on one of her braids. "Don't be so fussy, Naomi."

"I think I could do bananas better than hearts," Joy told Naomi.

Naomi sighed. "That would be so dumb."

As Joy poured lopsided pancake hearts, she wondered if Maya missed Shana. Would they ever be best friends again?

Maya was wondering the same thing.

# West 128th Street

Joy heard Sue and her father arguing as she opened the front door to the apartment.

"But you *promised* we'd go to St. Barts," Sue whined. "When you were fired, you said —"

"Stop saying I was fired," he shouted, interrupting her. "I was not fired. I was laid off."

Joy walked into the living room. Jake was playing on the floor between his fighting parents. When he saw Joy, he pushed himself to standing and ran to her. She opened her arms to him and asked, "Hey, Jakey, what's up?"

Sue answered the question. "We're not going to St. Barts."

Joy looked at her over Jake's head. "I know. I could hear you guys arguing from the hall. You were both yelling."

"I'm sorry about the vacation, Joy," her father said. "I'm a little stressed about this job thing —" He shot Sue an angry look. "— which I understand Sue has already told you about. Of course, I would prefer telling you these things myself. Anyway, I don't want to throw that kind of money down the drain."

"A new set of golf clubs is *not* throwing money down the drain?" asked Sue.

"How about your health club membership?" he shot back.

"A membership is a way to *save* money," she argued.

He laughed bitterly. "Spending two thousand dollars a year is *saving* money? Could you explain that, please?"

As they argued, Jake looked from one parent to the other, his little face scrunched with concern.

Joy had a flashback. A dozen flashbacks at once. All of them of her parents arguing. And of being scared.

"I'm taking Jake out," she announced.

Her father nodded an okay.

Sue said, "Don't forget his bottle." And they went back to arguing.

Joy carried Jake into his room to get his jacket, took a half-filled bottle out of the refrigerator, pulled the stroller into the hall, and left.

As the elevator carried them down to the lobby she told Jake, "We'll go to the playground. Then we'll go hang out in a café."

She pushed him on the kid swings and rode the slide with him on her lap. Jake laughed all the way down and wanted to do it again. And again.

After three slides, she put him back in his stroller and gave him his bottle. She checked out the playground crowd. Some moms and a few dads with a kid or two were hanging out. There were some babysitters, like herself, with young charges.

Jake let out a wail and held out his empty bottle.

Joy took it. "Let's go find you some more milk and crackers, Jakey. I know just the place."

As she was pushing the stroller up West Eighth Street, the black lace at the hem of her bell-bottoms caught in the wheel. She stopped to get it out. Jake whimpered. He was thirsty, hungry, and, she could smell, needed a diaper change. I forgot to bring diapers, she realized as she pulled at the lace.

A woman walking around the stroller said to her companion, "I don't understand why anyone would trust a baby to someone who dressed like that."

"Maybe it's her baby," commented the other woman.

"Worse," said the first woman. "Dreadful."

The lace ripped free and Joy stood up. She looked after the women. One of them, glancing over her shoulder, met Joy eye to eye.

"Mind your own business," Joy shouted to her.

Jake's whimper morphed into a wail.

She squatted beside his stroller. "I'm sorry, Jakey. I'm sorry." He looked at her, grabbed for her dangling skull earring, and stopped crying.

I took him for a walk to get him away from people who shout, Joy thought, then I shouted. But I hate that woman. The way I dress has nothing to do with my being a good or a bad babysitter. Why do people judge other people by such superficial things?

On the way into the deli, Joy spotted her reflection in the window — long, black lace bell-bottoms, scoop-necked black top, short black leather jacket, black lipstick and nails, a black choker.

Inside she bought a pint of milk, a box of crackers, diapers for Jake, and an apricot roll for herself. As the clerk took her money, Joy wondered, Does he think I dress weird, too?

As soon as Joy left the store, she filled Jake's bottle with milk and opened the box of crackers. She gave him one cracker for each hand and stuck the apricot roll in her pocket. Jake's smelly diaper had ruined her appetite and reminded her of her next problem. Where could she change a baby's diaper? She remembered seeing a diaper-changing station in the restroom of the mega-bookstore. She was headed there when her cell phone rang.

If it's Maya or Carolyn, will I tell them that we're not going to St. Barts? That Dad and Sue are fighting? That my dad lost his job? Even as Joy thought the questions, she knew the answers. No. No. No.

But it wasn't Maya or Carolyn calling. It was her father.

"I'm sorry that you came in when we were arguing," he said. "Sue and I have a lot to work out."

"Jake heard it, too," Joy observed.

"Well, he's just a baby. I'm also sorry I had to cancel the trip to St. Barts. I know you were looking forward to it."

Joy brushed Jake's hair off his forehead. It would have been fun to show him the ocean. "Aren't you and Sue going to that brunch? It's why I came down to babysit."

"Sue went alone. I'm not in the mood."

Jake started fussing again.

"Is Jake okay?" her father asked, concerned.

"His diaper's dirty," she explained. "And I think he wants to go home."

"So come."

When Joy got back to the apartment, she handed her smelly half brother over to her father.

"I'm going back to Mom's," she announced. "I have homework to do."

"You could do it here," he offered. "Jake won't bother you. He's going down for his nap soon."

"My books are at home." She kissed Jake on the cheek. "See you, pal."

Jake looked up at his big sister with big, round brown eyes. Joy kissed him again and left.

As she walked down the hall to the elevator, she thought, Jake and I have the same eyes.


Carolyn and her father were having brunch with their neighbors from Wyoming.

"Want one of my pancakes?" her father asked.

Carolyn looked down at her plate — cheese omelet, home fries, toast, chunks of pineapple and apple.

"No thanks. I already had pancakes today."

"Growing girl like you," Mr. Felder said, "I bet you can eat up a storm."

"I can," agreed Carolyn.

While they ate, the Felders listed all the touristy things they were doing in New York City.

"We're having a great time," Mr. Felder said. "First-class."

"Of course, it was very sad to go to Ground Zero," Mrs. Felder added. "But we wanted to do it. We felt we had to. It's a way to remember all those people who died."

Mr. Felder nodded in agreement.

"One of my friends saw it happen," Carolyn told them. She described how Joy's bedroom window faced the World Trade Center and that she'd seen the planes hit and the towers fall.

They asked Carolyn how she met Joy and wanted to know all about the photography workshop. While Carolyn chatted with the Felders, she noticed that her father was quiet and not eating much. Does he wish he was with M. G. instead of us? she wondered.

Later, as they all left the restaurant, Mrs. Felder announced that she and her husband were going to the Metropolitan Museum. She looked from Carolyn to her father. "Anyone want to come with us? As I've learned from you, it's just across the park."

"I have some work to catch up on," Carolyn's father told them. He turned to Carolyn. "You could go."

In her mind's eye, Carolyn saw her homework To Do list. *Book report for English. Two pages of math problems. Reread chapter 15 in history book.* "I have a lot of homework."

Mr. Felder smiled approvingly at Carolyn. "You always were a conscientious girl. And a good student. Your mother would be proud of you."

Mrs. Felder sighed. "We all miss her so."

"We sure do," added Mr. Felder.

Carolyn hugged and kissed them good-bye and the Felders went off toward the park. Carolyn and her father went in the opposite direction.

"We need groceries," he commented as they walked along Amsterdam Avenue. "Do you want to come with me, or do you need to get started on that homework?"

"I should probably get started," she agreed. Thinking about all she had to do made her feel tired. *I only had five hours of sleep last night,* she remembered. *I'll go to bed early tonight.*

"We could go to a movie tonight," her father said, interrupting her thoughts of bedtime. "When you've finished your homework."

"I don't think I'll have time," she answered.

*I bet he wishes he could go to the movies with M. G.,* she thought. *Maybe I should tell him that it's okay with me if he does. Maybe it would put him in a better mood.*

"If you want to go out with Dr. Geng tonight," she said, "it's okay with me. I have a lot to do."

He shook his head and answered without looking at her. "Dr. Geng and I aren't dating anymore. We're still colleagues, but we're not —" He let the sentence trail off.

"Sorry," she said, even though she wasn't.

"It's probably better this way," he said.

They'd reached the front of their building. "I'll get those chocolate-covered cookies you like," he said. "Milk chocolate or dark?"

"Dark," she answered.

"All right. See you soon." He turned and walked slowly down the street.

As Carolyn walked into the building, she felt a grin spread across her face. She hadn't liked the idea of her father with M. G. M. G. who might marry him someday. M. G. who might try to replace her mother. So it was good that he stopped seeing M. G. Right?

By the time she went to bed that night, she wasn't so sure that it was good. Her father seemed sad and was more absentminded than ever. During dinner, he'd asked her the same questions about school and the arts festival that he'd asked her while they were making dinner.

When the phone rang he had startled and rushed to answer it. He looked disappointed when he said that it was Maya calling her. He wishes it was M. G. calling him, Carolyn had thought as she took the phone.

By the time Carolyn was on the bus for school the next morning, she felt guilty. Her father had started being happy after he met Dr. Geng. He'd bought new clothes, danced at the party at the museum, went to the park at lunchtime, and whistled happy tunes. He was relaxed. Then I let him know I was upset that he was dating. That I didn't want to have anything to do with Dr. Geng. He broke up with M. G. because of me. Now he's back to being like he became after Mom died — sad and tense. It's my fault. I made him feel bad about having a girlfriend.

After the darkroom session on Saturday, Beth said, "All right, gang, we're going to do portraits. I want all of you to take two rolls of film of one person. Get up close and personal." She held up a print. "Like this."

*Close-up of Shana glaring at the camera.*

She held up another print. "And this."

*Close-up of Charlie's sister smiling at the camera.*

"Serious, honest portraits," she concluded. "Got it?"

Joy remembered the honest pictures she'd taken of baby Jake.

*Close-up of Jake crying.*

*Medium shot of Jake with food all over his face.*

Carolyn remembered the portraits she'd taken of Maya's grandmother, Josie. And the ones Maya had taken of Shana for the last photo workshop. Shana didn't mind Maya taking her picture then.

"We did that assignment for the first workshop," Joy reminded Beth.

"Did you shoot in black and white?" Beth asked. "And did we print them ourselves?"

Joy shook her head.

"I rest my case," concluded Beth with a little bow in Joy's direction.

Joy rolled her eyes at Maya as if to say, You can't win.

Maya leaned toward her and whispered, "Can I take your picture?"

"Okay," Joy whispered back. Why does Maya want to take my picture? she wondered. I'm not pretty or even interesting looking.

Beth showed them portraits by Richard Avedon. For each photo, she asked them what they learned about the person from looking at the photo.

Later, when they left the media center together, Maya asked Joy again if she could take her picture. "I'd like to do it now."

"Now?" repeated Joy. "Today?"

Maya nodded. "Remember when you brought us up to the roof at your Dad's place? I'd like to shoot there."

"Can I help?" Carolyn asked. "I can stay out until six as long as I'm with you guys."

"And as long as you let your dad know where you are and what you're doing every minute," teased Joy.

"I don't have to do that anymore," Carolyn announced.

"Since when?" asked Maya.

"Since he has a girlfriend," Joy answered for Carolyn. She grinned at her. "You can thank M. G. for your freedom. That's a lot more than Sue's ever given me."

"He already broke up with M. G.," Carolyn told them. "I think because I was so upset about him having a girlfriend."

"Oops," said Joy.

"I feel awful," continued Carolyn. "Do you think I should tell him it's really okay with me?"

"Is it?" asked Maya.

"I don't want him to be unhappy because of me," answered Carolyn. "He's so down in the dumps."

"Down in the dumps?" repeated Joy. "An expression from Grandpa, no doubt."

"No doubt," agreed Carolyn.

I bet Carolyn's father isn't as down in the dumps as my father, thought Joy. I hope that he and Sue don't argue in front of Carolyn and Maya. I hope they're not even home.

They weren't. No one was home.

Carolyn didn't want to talk about her father and M. G. anymore. She made a 360-degree turn in the middle of the living room. "I love this apartment!" she exclaimed. "It's so cheerful and *big*. Do you miss it when you're at your mom's?"

"No," answered Joy.

"Course not," said Carolyn feeling stupid. "That's also a super apartment."

A dark thought shadowed Joy's mind. The apartment was a rental. An expensive rental. Would her father be able to afford it if he didn't find another job soon?

"Do you want something to eat?" she asked Maya and Carolyn.

Maya glanced out the window. The light was beautiful. "Let's take the photos first."

Maya watched Joy check herself out in the mirror over the couch. Black bell-bottoms and a stretchy black top, dark red lipstick, white powder, spiking gel in her hair. There are times when Joy seems so mysterious, thought Maya. Like she's full of secrets. Will I learn anything new about her?

Joy turned from the mirror. "You want me like this?" she asked Maya. "Or should I change?"

"I could do one roll like you are now and the next one in a different outfit," answered Maya.

"That'd be okay," agreed Joy.

"Beth said the pictures should be honest," Carolyn reminded Joy.

Joy faced her. "You don't think this is honestly who I am?"

"I guess," answered Carolyn. But she was thinking, sometimes I don't know who you are, Joy. Especially when you keep changing how you look.

The girls went up to the roof and Maya started to shoot.

*Joy, hands on hips. New York City skyline behind her. Click.*

*Joy sneering. Click.*

"Relax," Maya directed. "But no smiles."

"Not for Goth," agreed Carolyn.

*Joy smiling wickedly. Click.*

"I thought that might be a way to get her to smile," Maya whispered to Carolyn.

"Me, too," admitted Carolyn.

*Joy lying on the roof, arms outstretched. Click.*

"Roll's done," announced Maya.

They went down to the apartment. Joy showered the gunk out of her hair and the makeup off her face. She came out in her terry-cloth bathrobe. "What should I wear next?"

"I like the denim skirt Jay-Cee made for you," suggested Carolyn.

"With a white top," added Maya. "For something really different from Goth."

Joy put on the skirt and a white T-shirt, blew her short hair soft and straight, and finished off the look with pink lipstick and a little blush. She smiled primly at Maya and Carolyn. "Do I project sweetness?" she asked.

"Totally," answered Carolyn. "You look great in pink and blue."

"We're using black-and-white film," Joy reminded her.

They went back up to the roof. As Maya was finishing off the roll, Joy worried about going back down to her dad's apartment. Would her dad and Sue be home? she wondered. What would be going on when she walked in with her friends?

*Joy in profile looking thoughtfully into the distance. Click.*

Sue was in the kitchen with Jake when the three girls came back to the apartment.

"Joy," Sue called cheerfully. "Hi, Carolyn. Hi, Maya. I saw the backpacks and thought, Joy and her friends have dropped by. Yay! I'll have some company."

They all said "Hi" back.

Jake banged on his high-chair tray for Joy's attention. She went to him and tapped her fingernails on the tray. He grinned up at her and grabbed at her fingers.

"Sometimes a girl just needs some girl company," Sue told Maya and Carolyn. "Want some sodas? I have diet." She laughed. "But you two don't have to worry about diet anything, do you? You're nice and slim. Not like Joy and me. We are constantly fighting the battle of the bulge." She giggled. "I guess it's an example of 'like stepmother, like stepdaughter.'" She put an arm around Joy's shoulders. "Right?"

Wrong, thought Joy. You're the diet freak, not me. Jake threw his sippy cup over the side of the high chair.

Maya picked it up and handed it to him. He threw it right back down. This time Maya caught it midair. He clapped with delight at her trick.

"Joy looks so good in that outfit, doesn't she?" Sue gushed. "In some ways I like it better on you than Goth. But there is one good thing about that Goth style. Black slenderizes," Sue said. "White makes you look bulky."

Carolyn and Maya exchanged a glance. Poor Joy. Her stepmother was so weird.

"Da-da-da!" Jake announced. He pointed his cup toward the kitchen door before dropping it into Maya's waiting hands.

Oh, great, thought Joy. Just in case Sue hasn't embarrassed me enough, now we have down-in-the-dumps Dad.

"Looks like we have a houseful," he said for starters. "I'm so glad you're finally bringing your friends around, Joy."

"My friends have been around, Dad," explained Joy. "You just weren't here when they came. You were at work."

He shot her a glance that said I hope you didn't tell your friends that I am out of a job. "It's Saturday, isn't it? Aren't I usually here on Saturdays?"

"You're here on Saturdays, Sundays, Mondays, Tuesdays . . ." Sue began. A glare from her husband stopped her in mid-week.

Tense vibes are bouncing all over this apartment, thought Maya, and it's really upsetting Joy. We should get her out of here. Fast. She patted Joy on the arm. "Are you going back uptown?"

Joy turned to Maya and nodded that she was. Maya saw Joy as a black-and-white photo.

*Close-up of Joy, sad and worried.*

# Battery Park

Sunday morning, Maya woke up to sunlight. I'm going to stay outside *all* day, she vowed. I'll call Jay-Cee and see if she wants to Rollerblade. But not Delores. And not Shana.

Maya closed her eyes and thought about Shana. This was just the kind of Sunday they would have spent together. Shana would show up around 9:00 in the morning. They'd make pancakes for her little sisters and spend the rest of the day in the park Rollerblading and hanging out with friends. Around 6:00, Shana would go home with her and stay for dinner. It would be 9:00 at night before Shana went home — twelve hours after she arrived.

"Time to get up!"

Maya opened her eyes and saw Shana standing over her. She sat up. "I was just thinking about you."

"And here I am." Shana arched an eyebrow. "You must be psychic."

As Maya got up, Shana bent over and peeked under the bed.

"What are you looking for?"

Shana grinned up at her mischievously and

paused before answering. "Joy-less and Red. Thought you might be hiding them someplace."

"Girl, when are you gonna stop giving me a hard time about them?" Maya asked. "Is that what you came over for?"

"I came over to make dinosaur pancakes for Naomi. And to tell you I'm moving to Brooklyn."

"You're moving? How come?"

Shana sat on the bed and pulled a pillow onto her lap. "To live with my aunt while my mom's in the hospital."

"Is she sick?" asked Maya, alarmed. "What's wrong?"

"Yeah, she's sick," said Shana. "In the head. She's got this mental problem. All her life, my aunt says. So now they're gonna try to fix it with drugs and stuff." She arched her eyebrow again. "They're going to *observe* her. Man. I could tell the doctors lots about my mother. I've been *observing* her all my life."

Maya sat on the bed, cross-legged, facing Shana. "Maybe that's why she hurt you and stuff," she said. "Because of her mental problems."

"I guess."

"Shana, I'm sorry I didn't figure out what was going on. I could have helped. I mean, maybe I could have helped."

Shana fluffed up the pillow. "You mean you should have known my mom hit me because you're supposed to know stuff? Like your grandmother?"

Maya nodded.

Shana put the pillow behind her head and leaned back on the bed. "You didn't know, M, because I didn't want you to." She tapped her head and grinned. "I got a powerful mind, too."

Maya smiled back. "I know."

Naomi came in, saw Shana, shouted "You're here!," and did a flying leap on top of her. Hannah and Piper came in behind Naomi and added themselves to the people-pile.

Shana tickled the three girls. "How would you like to eat pterodactyls today?"

"Yes! Yes!" shouted Hannah.

"*And* T-rex," added Naomi.

Shana sat up. "Let's do it!"

"I'm getting dressed," Maya announced to anyone who cared.

Piper followed Hannah, Naomi, and Shana out of the room. "I want hearts. I want hearts," she chanted. "Not funny hearts like Joy makes. Good ones."

Carolyn was having Sunday breakfast with her father.

A shaft of sunlight cut across the counter. "It's a great day, Dad."

He turned the page of the paper. "I hope you'll be spending some time outside."

"You, too," she said.

He looked at her over his reading glasses. "I'm going to catch up on some work today."

Carolyn thought, If Dad were still dating M. G., he wouldn't work on Sunday. He'd relax and do fun things. He broke up with Dr. Geng because of me. If he never finds another love in his life, it will be my fault. She took a swig of orange juice. It's not fair to him. I have to do something about this situation. Now!

"Dad, I'm sorry that you aren't going out with M. G. — Dr. Geng — anymore. I shouldn't have said I didn't want to ever do stuff with her and everything. You're right. You need a girlfriend. I was wrong. I —"

He put up a hand. "Whoa. Wait a minute here. Do you think Maxine and I broke up because you were upset?" he asked. "That you got between us?"

She nodded.

He smiled sadly. "You're missing a piece of pertinent information here. *I* didn't break it off with Maxine. She broke up with me."

M. G. broke up with him? thought Carolyn. She had walked hand in hand with him in Central Park. Went out on dates. Even traveled with him in Thailand. Then she broke up with him. Why? The answer was clear.

"It's still my fault, Dad," Carolyn explained to her father. "She broke up with you *after* she met me. I wasn't exactly friendly. Even Joy noticed it."

Her father leaned toward her. "Carolyn, you had nothing to do with it. An old boyfriend of Maxine's showed up, and they got back together. Moreover, I don't think I'm the kind of man she's looking for. As

your grandfather would say, 'I wasn't her cup of tea.'"
He patted Carolyn's hand. "In any case, it's not your
fault. Do you understand that?"

She nodded, even though she wasn't sure that
she did.

"By the way," he said. "I have a present for you."

"You do?"

He nodded. "I've made some inquiries and figured out that we can afford it, say once every two
weeks."

"Afford what, Dad?"

"Guess."

Her mind churned over ideas — eating out more
often, going to more plays and movies. She didn't
think any of them was it.

He took a sip of coffee and watched her thinking. "Give up?"

She nodded.

"Riding sessions at Claremont Stables! I explained that you are an experienced rider. They'll try
you in the ring, but then you should be able to ride in
the park."

Riding in New York City! Did she want to? She remembered riding at home in Wyoming. Mandy and
her riding across miles and miles of open fields.
Whole days working the horses with her mother and
grandparents.

"I never thought of riding in New York," she told
her father.

"Well, you can now," he said proudly. "Once they

get to know you at Claremont, maybe they'll let you help out with some of the boarder horses and not charge —" He interrupted himself to ask her. "What's wrong? You don't seem very enthusiastic. I thought you missed riding."

Carolyn was thinking about Jolly and Maximillian and how they lived in small stalls without yards. "I do miss riding," she explained, "but I don't want to ride in New York. Riding is about the ranch and Tailgate. Besides, my New York friends don't ride."

New images replaced the Wyoming riding images. Rollerblading in Maya's skates around the fountain in front of the Plaza Hotel and through Central Park. "What I really want to do is Rollerblade, Dad. That's what Maya and her friends do."

"You know that I don't think Rollerblading in a busy city is safe."

"It's safer than riding a horse in a busy city," she argued. "Besides, I'd wear a helmet and those arm and knee guards."

"And you wouldn't go on the streets?"

"I wouldn't."

He took another sip of coffee. Finally, he said, "Maybe we could use the money I earmarked for riding to buy you Rollerblades."

"Yes!" she shouted. She jumped off the stool and hugged him. "Can we go now? I know where to get them and everything."

"Do you think I can have another cup of coffee first?" he asked, laughing. "Maybe finish my breakfast?"

*     *     *

Joy came in from outside with the Sunday *New York Times* and breakfast takeout from the diner — two egg-and-cheese sandwiches, one coffee light for her mother, and fresh-squeezed orange juice for her.

Her mother took the paper from her. "How is it out there?"

Joy put the coffee and a sandwich in front of her. "Nice."

Her mother flipped the lid off the coffee cup. "What's your plan for the day?"

Joy sat down. "Don't have one yet."

They ate and read the paper. Joy heard her mother mumble to herself, "It's hopeless."

Joy took the last bite of her egg sandwich. "What's hopeless?"

Her mother closed the business section of the paper and pushed it aside. "The economy. It's killing business — *my* business." She took off her reading glasses and looked around the big kitchen. "We might have to give this place up. Get something smaller."

"I thought we owned this apartment."

"Us and the bank. There's a monthly mortgage payment plus a hefty maintenance fee and taxes."

Joy sat back and stared at her mother. "I thought you made a lot of money doing all those commercials."

"I used to. But I don't now." She raised one finger. "That is the number of commercials I have lined up. Last year at this time I had —" She held up the fingers of both hands. "Count them — ten. I had to let two people go last week."

Does Mom know that Dad is having money problems, too? Joy wondered. That he lost his job?

Her mother laughed. "Good thing your father is rich. He's going to have to pay the rest of your tuition."

While her mother went back to reading the paper and eating her breakfast, Joy worried. What if Dad *can't* afford my tuition? What if he can't afford *his* apartment, either? Where will we all live? Where will *I* live?

Joy's cell phone rang. The call, she saw, was from Carolyn. Maybe we'll do something together today, she thought. Anything is better than sitting around the apartment worrying about money.

"Guess what?" Carolyn said excitedly. "I'm getting Rollerblades today. Now. Then Maya's coming over, and we're going to skate. And Shana might come."

Joy remembered the one time she tried Rollerblading. She was nine and all the girls in her class were getting them. Her mother bought her a pair. The first time she tried them, she fell. Everyone laughed because of the funny way she lost her footing. Even her mother was smiling. Joy pretended she thought it was funny, too. But after that, whenever she put on the skates, she was terrified she'd fall again, so of course she did. Again and again.

A few weeks later, she told her mother that she didn't want to skate anymore. Her mother had said, "Maybe you're just not built for Rollerblading." And the skates — two sizes too small by now — were in the back of her closet.

"Do you have Rollerblades?" Carolyn was asking.

"I used to," answered Joy. "But they're too small. I don't like it that much, anyway."

"You should try it again. Come over now and we can shop for skates together. We're going to go to Riverside Park and skate all the way downtown. You have to come."

Joy remembered how easily Carolyn skated. It came naturally to her. Maya, too, was graceful on skates. Skating all the way downtown would be a breeze for them. For her it would be torture. And embarrassing — especially if Shana came.

"I have a bike," Joy said. "I can bike while you skate." She pictured her bike in with dozens of others in the bike room in the building's basement. She hadn't ridden it in more than a year. "I might have to get air in the tires. But there's a place near here."

"Great," said Carolyn. "See you at my place. In an hour. Okay?"

As Joy closed her phone she wondered, who pays for my cell phone? Mom? Or Dad? Will I have to give it up?

The dinosaur and heart pancakes were inside the three little sisters' bellies. Shana was making regular pancakes for Maya and herself.

"Who called before?" Shana asked. "Was it Joyless or Red?"

"Red," answered Maya. "She's getting Rollerblades today and wants *us* to blade with her."

"I'm busy today," Shana said.

"Come on, Shana," Maya protested. "Don't be like that. Maybe Jay-Cee will come."

Shana flipped the pancakes. "Jay-Cee's sewing all day. She got some orders for those halters. Anyway, Alex and his brother are going to help me move my stuff to Brooklyn. His brother's borrowing a car from somebody."

Maya was about to offer to help Shana move when she got the feeling that Shana didn't want her. A wave of unhappiness rippled through Maya. Shana would rather be alone with Alex and his brother, she thought, and I'm jealous. Is this how Shana feels about Carolyn and Joy?

She held out two plates for pancakes. "If you're living in Brooklyn, when will I see you?"

Shana shrugged her shoulders. "Don't know. When you come to Brooklyn, I guess." She piled pancakes on the plate.

"Come on, Shana. You have to come back to the neighborhood sometimes. All your friends are here. We can still have sleepovers and stuff. With Jay-Cee."

Shana looked sideways at Maya. A slow smile worked at the edges of her mouth. "Sure. Why not?"

Maya smiled back.

Carolyn and Joy waited for Maya in Riverside Park. Skaters, bikers, walkers, runners, and people pushing strollers went up and down the wide, paved path along the Hudson River.

The two girls stood at the railing and checked out the houseboats moored at the 79th Street Boat Basin.

"Some people live on these boats year-round," observed Joy. She pointed to one that looked more like a shack than a boat. "That one couldn't go anywhere if it wanted to. But someone lives there." A man carrying a small child walked out onto the deck of the shabby houseboat as if to prove her right. "I would never want to live on a houseboat."

"Why?" asked Carolyn.

"First of all, they're not very big. Anyway, these aren't. And second, they're in water, which means they must rock a lot. I'd hate that feeling."

Carolyn leaned on the railing and rolled her new wheels back and forth under herself. "I was just thinking how much fun it would be to live on a houseboat. I think it'd be cozy in one of those. I'd enjoy that rocking feeling. It's like being in the saddle. Or being rocked when you were a baby." She stopped scissoring her Rollerblades and pointed uptown. "Here comes Maya!"

Maya saw Carolyn and Joy and waved. Carolyn skated off to meet her. Joy watched the two friends happily spin each other around. Should I stay here and wait for them? she wondered. Or should I ride over there? Before she could decide which to do, the two skaters came to her.

"Joy, I have contact sheets of the pictures I took of you," Maya announced. "They look good."

Carolyn leaned on Joy's shoulder. "I can't wait to see."

They all sat on a bench facing the river and Maya handed Joy a contact sheet and a loupe for magnifying the image. Joy held the loupe over the contact sheet and saw herself in one little square after another. She looked over at Maya and said, "I don't like any of these pictures."

A flash of disappointment crossed Maya's face.

Joy saw it. "Not because of how you took them, Maya," she said. "You're a good photographer. It's just that I never like pictures of myself."

Carolyn moved the loupe over the contact sheet. "You look sad in a lot of these. But I think it's because of the Goth look."

I don't look sad because of the way I dress, thought Joy. I look sad because I *am* sad a lot of the time.

Maya handed Joy another contact sheet. "Here's the second one. You have on that denim skirt and white top in this set."

Joy looked at the sheet of little pictures. "Do you think Sue's right?" she asked. "Does white make me look bulkier?"

"No!" answered Maya emphatically. "Your stepmother is a little weird about weight, don't you think?"

"Definitely," agreed Carolyn.

Joy nodded. "She's always watching what I eat and commenting on it. It just makes me want to eat more." She pointed her index finger at Carolyn. "Sue weighs herself so much, the tread on the scale is all worn off."

"Really?" said Carolyn.

Joy laughed. "CK, you're just too easy to catch. . . ."

"It could have been true," protested Carolyn.

"You're right," agreed Joy. "I should check the scale." She took the first contact sheet back from Carolyn and looked at the twenty-four frames again. I look big on top whether I wear black or white, she decided. I *am* big on top. Period.

Carolyn squinted at the pictures on the second contact sheet. Joy handed her the loupe.

"Well, I think you look great in both contact sheets, Joy," Maya said. "You should dress however you want."

"Actually, I am getting sick of Goth," admitted Joy. She looked down at her black T-shirt and jeans. "And always wearing black. I think it's depressing me."

"You? Depressed?" said Carolyn.

Joy looked at her blankly.

Carolyn grinned back at Joy and said, "Gotcha!"

Joy smiled. "But I like having a style," she continued. She pointed to the second contact sheet. "Dressing like this is a nothing style."

"I think it's a real style," said Maya. "Simple, direct, no nonsense."

Maybe Carolyn and Maya were right, thought Joy. Maybe I should dress more simply. "If I drop

Goth," she said, "my parents and Sue will think I did it for them."

"Don't worry about them or what they think," counseled Maya. "Do what feels like you."

I'm not sure what that is, thought Joy.

Carolyn skated a turn in front of them. "Come on. Let's go. I'm dying to use my skates."

Maya stood up and raised her right arm. "All the way to Battery Park!" she vowed.

"How far is that?" asked Carolyn.

"I looked it up on the Internet before I left," said Joy. "It's about five miles from here."

"And there are no cars," promised Maya. "On any of it."

If I bike slowly, Joy thought as they started out, I can stay with them.

There was a breeze off the river. To Carolyn's right, a seagull cawed and swooped toward the water. To her left, skyscrapers loomed. Mandy will not believe this, she thought. We have to do it again when she comes to visit. She can rent skates. I bet she'd be great at Rollerblading. We'll have so much fun. Dark thoughts pushed away Carolyn's happy daydream. What if Mandy doesn't like Maya and Joy? Will Joy's sarcasm bother her? A new question joined the others. What if Joy and Maya don't like Mandy?

Joy braked her bike in front of a huge, docked ship. "That's the USS *Intrepid*," she told Carolyn.

"It's a museum now," Maya told her. "My class went in fourth grade."

"My fourth-grade class went, too," added Joy, happy at the coincidence.

"Maybe you were both there on the same day," suggested Carolyn.

Maya and Joy exchanged a smile.

"Maybe," said Maya.

They skated and biked away from the *Intrepid* toward downtown Manhattan.

As Maya skated slowly along, she remembered the class trip to the *Intrepid*. It was the year Loreen had convinced all the girls in the class that Maya was a snob, and they all had snubbed her. But Shana had stayed her friend.

Carolyn turned to see where Maya was. Maya picked up speed and rolled up beside them.

Joy shifted down so Maya wouldn't have to work so hard to keep up with her. Maya smiled a thank-you. It was so wonderful to just be with her friends, enjoying a beautiful spring day.

As the three girls continued rolling downtown, Joy thought about her uncle Brett and the bike rides she'd taken with him. She wished he hadn't died. She wished he was around to meet her new friends. If Uncle Brett was alive, I would have done the black-and-white portrait assignment of him, she decided.

"Did you decide who to shoot for the portrait assignment?" Maya asked her. A little chill ran across the top of Joy's head. Sometimes it seemed like Maya knew what she was thinking.

"Remember that mystery writer who lives across the hall from me?" Joy asked.

The bikeway widened, and Carolyn rolled up on the other side of Joy's bike. "Paget Sanders," she said. "I liked her. She didn't tell your mother about Wren and those guys crashing your party."

"Anyway, she said I could photograph her," reported Joy. "She wants me to do it in her writing room because that's where she spends all her time."

"Have you ever seen it?" asked Maya.

"No," answered Joy.

Carolyn dropped behind to let a faster skater pass them, then rolled back up beside Joy. "It should be interesting to see where a mystery writer works," she said. "I wonder if she has framed covers of her books all over the walls."

Joy pulled ahead to make room for another bike. When the three friends were side by side, she said, "I'll let you know about the covers. She told me once that her books were translated into Chinese."

Now Maya dropped back to let an approaching Rollerblader pass. "CK, who are you going to take pictures of?" she shouted.

"Ivy," Carolyn called back to her. "She already said I could."

"You already took her," observed Joy.

Maya was rolling beside them again. "She took those in color," she said.

"That's right," agreed Carolyn. "I want to see how

Ivy looks in black and white." She didn't tell her friends that the real reason was that she wanted to spend more time with Ivy. That Ivy was the most interesting adult she'd met in New York City.

They stopped to buy cold drinks from a street vendor in front of low buildings with a big sign reading CHELSEA PIERS. Carolyn turned to Joy and asked, "What's Chelsea Piers?"

"It's a sports center," answered Joy. "It's huge. It takes up about six blocks." She patted Carolyn on the shoulder. "Hey, cowgirl, they even have horseback riding there. They call it the Equestrian Center."

"Fan-cy," observed Carolyn.

They skated and biked past Chelsea Piers with its banners advertising a field house, sky rink, sports center, and golf club. When they reached Battery Park, Joy leaned her bike against a tree, Maya and Carolyn took off their skates, and the three friends sat on a bench facing the Statue of Liberty.

"She's beautiful," said Carolyn. "It must be so neat to go up in the crown and look out."

"You've never been?" asked Joy.

Carolyn shook her head.

"I went on a class trip," Joy and Maya said in unison. They turned and grinned at each other.

Carolyn pulled out her camera. "I want to take your picture," she said. "Just like that."

*Close-up of Maya and Joy grinning at each other. Click.*

On the class trip to the Statue of Liberty, Shana

and I had a great time Maya thought. We had each other. We had a good time this morning, too. It was almost like it used to be. Memory snapshots flashed on Maya's mind screen.

*Shana fierce, standing up to Loreen.*

*Shana sad, sitting on her bed talking about her mother.*

*Shana smiling as she served dinosaur pancakes to the little sisters.*

Shana's still my friend, thought Maya. I'm glad she said she'd come around. And I will go to Brooklyn to see her. I want us to always be best friends. She's just not friends with two of my other friends. That's just how it is. But that's okay with me. Maybe it's even better. I'll have Shana to myself when I see her. *If* I see her.

Carolyn nudged her. "Earth to Maya."

Maya smiled. "Sorry. Just daydreaming." She looked from Carolyn to Joy. "Let's take a picture of all of us," she suggested.

"With the Statue of Liberty in the background," added Joy.

They went around to the back of the bench and leaned against it so Lady Liberty was behind them. Carolyn held her camera out at arm's length and pointed it at them.

"We have to be close so we're all in it," Maya said as she pulled Joy and Carolyn closer.

*Three friends — cheek to cheek — grinning at the camera. The Statue of Liberty in the background.*

*Click.*

# About the Author

Jeanne Betancourt lives and writes in New York City. She has written more than sixty books, including *My Name Is ~~Brain~~ Brian, Ten True Animal Rescue Stories*, and the popular Pony Pals series. Jeanne's work has been honored by many Children's Choice Awards. She is also an award-winning scriptwriter and has taught filmmaking to teens.

Trista Sordillo

*You've just finished Three Girls in the City #3.*
*Now picture this:*

# Three Girls
## in the City #4:

### CLOSE-UP

★ Joy has to face the facts. Her dad's out of work, and there will be no more credit cards, taxis, and spur-of-the-moment eating in restaurants for her. If she wants to have any fun at all, she's going to have to make a little money of her own. What a concept!

★ Maya's beginning to like having her old and new friends kind of separate. She sees Shana in Brooklyn, and Joy and Carolyn in Manhattan. Then Mandy, Carolyn's best friend from Wyoming, shows up and makes Shana like her. Why does this not feel good?

★ Carolyn thinks it will be great having her best friend Mandy come to visit from Wyoming. Sweet, shy Mandy. Carolyn will have to protect her from the harsher realities of New York City. But Mandy isn't sweet and shy anymore. She's changed, and she's changing how Carolyn feels about herself and her friends — but not in a good way. Then the lights go out all across the city and in the ensuing blackout chaos, Carolyn, Joy, Maya — and Mandy — are reminded what friendship's all about.

Look for Three Girls in the City #4:
*Close-Up,* in stores July 2004

About three girls with cameras sharing good times, hassles, laughter — and a citywide emergency.

Friendship, like the color black, goes with everything.

# Heartland

## Share Every Moment...

| | | | |
|---|---|---|---|
| ❏ BFF | 0-439-13020-4 | **#1: Coming Home** | $4.99 US |
| ❏ BFF | 0-439-13022-0 | **#2: After the Storm** | $4.99 US |
| ❏ BFF | 0-439-13024-7 | **#3: Breaking Free** | $4.99 US |
| ❏ BFF | 0-439-13025-5 | **#4: Taking Chances** | $4.99 US |
| ❏ BFF | 0-439-13026-3 | **#5: Come What May** | $4.99 US |
| ❏ BFF | 0-439-13035-2 | **#6: One Day You'll Know** | $4.99 US |
| ❏ BFF | 0-439-31714-2 | **#7: Out of the Darkness** | $4.99 US |
| ❏ BFF | 0-439-31715-0 | **#8: Thicker Than Water** | $4.99 US |
| ❏ BFF | 0-439-31716-9 | **#9: Every New Day** | $4.99 US |
| ❏ BFF | 0-439-31717-7 | **#10: Tomorrow's Promise** | $4.99 US |
| ❏ BFF | 0-439-33967-7 | **#11: True Enough** | $4.99 US |
| ❏ BFF | 0-439-33968-5 | **#12: Sooner or Later** | $4.99 US |
| ❏ BFF | 0-439-42508-5 | **#13: Darkest Hour** | $4.99 US |
| ❏ BFF | 0-439-42509-3 | **#14: Everything Changes** | $4.99 US |
| ❏ BFF | 0-439-42510-7 | **#15: Love Is a Gift** | $4.99 US |

**Available wherever you buy books, or use this order form.**

---

**Scholastic Inc., P.O. Box 7502, Jefferson City, MO 65102**

Please send me the books I have checked above. I am enclosing $_____ (please add $2.00 to cover shipping and handling). Send check or money order—no cash or C.O.D.s please.

Name_____ Birth date_____

Address_____

City_____ State/Zip_____

Please allow four to six weeks for delivery. Offer good in U.S.A. only. Sorry, mail orders are not available to residents of Canada. Prices subject to change.

**www.scholastic.com/kids**

# More Series You'll Fall in Love With

## Heartland™

Nestled in the foothills of Virginia, there's a place where horses come when they are hurt. Amy, Ty, and everyone at Heartland work together to heal the horses—and form lasting bonds that will touch your heart.

### The AMAZING DAYS of ABBY HAYES®

In a family of superstars, it's hard to stand out. But Abby is about to surprise her friends, her family, and most of all, herself!

Jody is about to begin a dream vacation on the wide open sea, traveling to new places and helping her parents with their dolphin research.

You can tag along with **Dolphin Diaries**

**Learn more at
www.scholastic.com/books**

Available Wherever Books Are Sold.

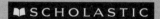
GIRLT1

# HAVE AN ABBY DAY!

Meet Abby Hayes, your typical amazing fifth grader and the star of a series that's as fresh and funny as Abby herself!

## Make your own calendar on Abby's Web site....
### www.scholastic.com/titles/abbyhayes

## Have you read them all?

- ❏ **Abby Hayes #1: Every Cloud Has a Silver Lining**
- ❏ **Abby Hayes #2: The Declaration of Independence**
- ❏ **Abby Hayes #3: Reach for the Stars**
- ❏ **Abby Hayes #4: Have Wheels, Will Travel**
- ❏ **Abby Hayes #5: Look Before You Leap**
- ❏ **Abby Hayes #6: The Pen Is Mightier Than the Sword**
- ❏ **Abby Hayes #7: Two Heads Are Better Than One**
- ❏ **Abby Hayes #8: The More, the Merrier**
- ❏ **Abby Hayes #9: Out of Sight, Out of Mind**
- ❏ **Abby Hayes #10: Everything New Under the Sun**
- ❏ **Abby Hayes #11: Too Close for Comfort**
- ❏ **Abby Hayes #12: Good Things Come in Small Packages**

## ◼ SCHOLASTIC

ABB0404

# Friends and adventures that set your heart free.

| | | | |
|---|---|---|---|
| ❑ 0-439-31947-1 | Dolphin Diaries #1: | Into the Blue | $4.99 US |
| ❑ 0-439-31948-X | Dolphin Diaries #2: | Touching the Waves | $4.99 US |
| ❑ 0-439-31949-8 | Dolphin Diaries #3: | Riding the Storm | $4.99 US |
| ❑ 0-439-31950-1 | Dolphin Diaries #4: | Under the Stars | $4.99 US |
| ❑ 0-439-31951-X | Dolphin Diaries #5: | Chasing the Dream | $4.99 US |
| ❑ 0-439-31952-8 | Dolphin Diaries #6: | Racing the Wind | $4.99 US |
| ❑ 0-439-44614-7 | Dolphin Diaries #7: | Following the Rainbow | $4.99 US |
| ❑ 0-439-44615-5 | Dolphin Diaries #8: | Dancing the Seas | $4.99 US |
| ❑ 0-439-44616-3 | Dolphin Diaries #9: | Leaving the Shallows | $4.99 US |

Available wherever you buy books, or use this order form.

**Scholastic Inc., P.O. Box 7502, Jefferson City, MO 65102**

Please send me the books I have checked above. I am enclosing $_____ (please add $2.00 to cover shipping and handling). Send check or money order—no cash or C.O.D.s please.

Name_____Birth date_____

Address_____

City_____State/Zip_____

Please allow four to six weeks for delivery. Offer good in U.S.A. only. Sorry, mail orders are not available to residents of Canada. Prices subject to change.

www.scholastic.com

DDBL0404